T0339999

SIMPLY IRRESISTIBLE

Berkley JAM titles by Jennifer Banash

THE ELITE
IN TOO DEEP
SIMPLY IRRESISTIBLE

SIMPLY IRRESISTIBLE

an ELITE novel

jennifer banash

BERKLEY JAM, NEW YORK

THE BERKLEY PUBLISHING GROUP
Published by the Penguin Group
Penguin Group (USA) Inc.
375 Hudson Street, New York, New York 10014, USA
Penguin Group (Canada), 90 Eglinton Avenue East, Suite 700, Toronto, Ontario M4P 2Y3, Canada
(a division of Pearson Penguin Canada Inc.)
Penguin Books Ltd., 80 Strand, London WC2R 0RL, England
Penguin Group Ireland, 25 St. Stephen's Green, Dublin 2, Ireland (a division of Penguin Books Ltd.)
Penguin Group (Australia), 250 Camberwell Road, Camberwell, Victoria 3124, Australia
(a division of Pearson Australia Group Pty. Ltd.)
Penguin Books India Pvt. Ltd., 11 Community Centre, Panchsheel Park, New Delhi—110 017, India
Penguin Group (NZ), 67 Apollo Drive, Rosedale, North Shore 0632, New Zealand
(a division of Pearson New Zealand Ltd.)
Penguin Books (South Africa) (Pty.) Ltd., 24 Sturdee Avenue, Rosebank, Johannesburg 2196,
South Africa

Penguin Books Ltd., Registered Offices: 80 Strand, London WC2R 0RL, England

This book is an original publication of The Berkley Publishing Group.

This is a work of fiction. Names, characters, places, and incidents either are the product of the author's imagination or are used fictitiously, and any resemblance to actual persons, living or dead, business establishments, events, or locales is entirely coincidental. The publisher does not have any control over and does not assume any responsibility for author or third-party websites or their content.

PRINTING HISTORY
Berkley JAM trade paperback edition / July 2009

Library of Congress Cataloging-in-Publication Data

Banash, Jennifer.
  Simply irresistible / Jennifer Banash. — Berkley JAM trade paperback ed.
    p. cm.
  Summary: With rivals Casey and Madison set to star in their own reality show, Madison ponders just how much of her life of privilege she wants to reveal, while Casey wonders how much of her luxurious New York City lifestyle is an illusion.
  ISBN 978-0-425-22783-1
  [1. Interpersonal relations—Fiction. 2. Wealth—Fiction. 3. Reality television programs—Fiction. 4. Identity—Fiction. 5. Dating (Social customs)—Fiction. 6. New York (N. Y.)—Fiction.] I. Title.

PZ7.B2176Sim 2009
[Fic]—dc22   2009011230

Fashion is a form of ugliness so intolerable that
we have to alter it every six months.

—OSCAR WILDE

plaza suite

Madison Macallister tossed her platinum blond hair back from her shoulders and snuggled more deeply into the cable-knit, ivory cashmere sweater that hung to her thighs. Her legs, encased in dark-washed skinny jeans so tight they appeared painted on, looked even longer and more stemlike than usual due to the stretchy denim that hugged every morsel of flesh from her nonexistent waist to her delicate ankles. *Skinny jeans are better than a fucking corset*, Mad thought as she leaned ever so slightly across the table and reached for the gleaming white and gold porcelain teapot. Not that she needed one. With her statuesque figure, glowing skin, green, slightly upturned eyes, and endless legs sheathed in winter white, knee-high suede Marc Jacobs boots, Madison Macallister was an icon of Upper East Side teen perfection—and she intended to keep it that way. And now that there were cameras in her face on a daily basis, obsessively roaming over and recording every inch of her envied and celebrated body, she couldn't afford to be careless about what she shoved in her mouth . . .

Madison poured the fragrant Lapsang souchong tea into a thin Spode teacup and raised it to her cranberry-glossed lips, ignoring the tall silver tray of tiny cucumber sandwiches and perfectly plump petit fours iced in sugary shades of lavender and rose, and looked around at the Plaza Hotel's freshly revamped dining room, sighing happily. When she was little, she'd read the *Eloise* books over and over again until their pages were stained and tattered, entranced by the antics of the precocious six-year-old who ran the lavish Upper East Side hotel as if it were her own private three-ring circus. After all, one of Madison's most beloved games as a child was pretending she *was* Eloise and that her stuffed monkey, Binky (who'd been loved so hard that his fur was missing in clumps), was Eloise's nanny. Madison would sit on the floor of her bedroom, a Fisher-Price telephone in her lap, and make pretend calls to room service, ordering—in a voice that was already slightly imperious—a cup of tea for Nanny and two sunflower seeds for her turtle Skipperdee, "And charge it, please. Thank you very much." Ever since Madison was five years old, Edie would take her to the Plaza each December for a "girls' day out," which usually included a long afternoon tea with plenty of sandwiches and cake, and then a mani-pedi at Elizabeth Arden, where Edie would proceed to pop Valium like a maniac, then babble nonsensically to Madison, the manicurist, the chair across the room—until Madison finally peeled Edie's Amex from her wallet and handed it over to the receptionist, who'd most definitely seen it all before.

Even though the Plaza had been freshened up a bit, Madison was relieved to see that nothing had really changed—there were still the same opulent, enticingly fragrant bouquets of flowers on every available surface; still the same garden-themed dining room with its airy, muted fabrics; still the same oil portrait of Eloise that hung just off the lobby, her small, mischievous face framed in softly glowing gold leaf. And December was the perfect time for a visit since the hotel was draped every holiday season without fail in sparkling white fairy lights and sweet-smelling pine garlands. A huge Christmas tree sat in the center of the dining room, snow-colored lights twinkling merrily, red velvet bows and gleaming silver balls affixed to its towering branches. Going to the Plaza with Edie for their holiday ritual was the only time Madison actually looked forward to spending with her annoying and Valium-obsessed mother all year long—until now.

Ever since Pulse TV had begun filming *De-Luxe*, a new reality show that was being touted as "a look inside the lives of the Upper East Side's REAL Gossip Girls," she'd barely had a moment to herself. Each day was filled with school, and then shoots that often stretched on well into the evening. Even now, the bright halogen lights shone in her face, making her glisten in a way she hoped wasn't too obvious on camera. Mad bit her bottom lip and prayed that the droplets of sweat that were threatening to make their way out of her pores wouldn't begin slowly rolling down her face. She wrinkled her brow as she remembered last week's shoot on the front steps of Meadowlark, how they had to constantly pause so the makeup artist could repeatedly blot Casey's disgustingly sweaty face. *At least I only sweat when there's some obnoxious, nuclear-powered light in my face,* Mad thought, wrinkling her brow and running the tip of her tongue surreptitiously over her teeth to be sure they were lipgloss-free. Casey was such a total disaster in every way possible that it was hard *not* to look good next to her on camera.

But if Mad had learned anything from seeing herself on tape, it was that the camera, with its sweeping, meticulous gaze, noticed absolutely everything—not to mention the fact that *De-Luxe* had no script to speak of. Not that it was a problem. If there was one thing that Mad knew she excelled at, it was inventing drama—and Madison Macallister practically had a Ph.D. in creating her own real-life soap operas. But she had always assumed, much like everyone else in the world, that the reality shows on Pulse were completely scripted, so she'd been surprised when the producer, Melanie, had been so hands-off with their dialogue from the very beginning,

"Why would we script it?" Melanie had barked the day Madison and Casey had arrived at the Pulse offices to sign their contracts. Melanie had pushed her tangle of red curls away from her pale face with exasperation before continuing, slamming her hand down on the table for emphasis. "Your real life is *better* than any crap we could make up!"

"Tell me something I *don't* know," Madison snapped, reaching over and grabbing the pen from Casey's hand and scrawling her signature at the bottom of the stack of pages piled in front of them.

Needless to say, the late nights and the grueling schedule were really screwing with both her social life *and* her academic performance, which as of late had been less than stellar—not that she was all that worried about it. Madison's problems, academic or otherwise, usually had a way of working themselves out—in her favor, of course . . . There was also the added headache of having to see the insufferable Ms. McCloy both in and out of school on a goddamn daily basis. Actually, she wasn't really *that* bad . . . Madison shook her head rapidly, trying to wipe the thought from her brain. God, all this holiday cheer and ho-ho-hoing was really getting to her. Well, at least she hadn't said it out loud . . .

Madison watched as her mother, Edith Spencer Macallister, brought her teacup to her lips, her expert maquillage and freshly blown-out blond shoulder-length mane obscured by a cloud of sweet-smelling white steam. Edie had taken to the cameras like a debutante to couture, and as a result her face looked tighter and even more plasticky than usual—thanks to the increasing visits to her dermatologist's office. Now that she and Antonio were officially an item, Edie, paranoid and random as ever, had decided that she needed all the help she could get in order to "keep up" with not only the TV cameras, but her younger man as well. To make matters worse, Edie had just embarked on some ridiculous detox diet where the only thing that would pass her seriously augmented lips for the next two weeks would be bottles of pee-colored lemon water mixed with cayenne pepper and maple syrup. The thought of such a regime was enough to make Madison almost regurgitate her Lapsang souchong all over the spotless white tablecloth.

Actually, she didn't know what was more nauseating—Edie's diet, or the fact that Edie and Antonio, a gorgeous Italian scout from Verve Model Management who had stopped Madison on the street in October, were now an item. Even though she'd decided pretty quickly that the life of a supermodel wasn't for her, what made the whole thing even harder to take was that she hadn't exactly felt the same way about Antonio. The night of Sophie's sweet sixteen he'd ended up going home with her mother, of all people. The thought was enough to make her gag reflex stop working permanently from bouts of constant dry heaving.

"Darling." Edie beamed, placing her cup back onto its saucer. "I don't want to ruin our time together today. But we do need to talk about something rather *serious.*" Edie's smile was replaced by a worried look as the camera moved in for a close-up. *Crap*, Mad thought, exhaling loudly and looking down at her tea. *Here we go . . .* "I've spoken to your academic advisor at Meadowlark and your recent grades are completely unacceptable."

Edie's voice was suddenly as brittle as the icicles hanging from the tops of the buildings lining Fifth Avenue—and every bit as cold. The gold Kenneth Jay Lane bracelets lining her wrists jingled with a tinny, metallic sound as she waved her hands expansively for emphasis. "If you're going to have even the *faintest* shot at getting into Harvard, you are going to have to step things up. And if you don't," Edie paused to dig in her beige Chanel tote for an amber-colored prescription bottle, swallowing a small, yellow pill before continuing, "then I'll be forced to pull you from the show—no exceptions. You need to concentrate on your *future* for a change."

Madison rolled her eyes and picked up a small, pink cookie, biting down angrily. *Screw calories.* As the shiny icing broke between her teeth like crusted snow, Mad knew that as much as it killed her to admit it, for once her mother was actually right. She had been ignoring her schoolwork—along with most everything else in her cluttered, jumbled, seriously over-committed life. But it was kind of hard to concentrate on the pointlessness of world history or algebra when total stardom was waiting just around the corner . . .

"Edie, *cara.* There you are." Madison whipped her head around at the sound of Antonio's mellifluous Italian accent, her cheeks bulging with unchewed pastry. Mad swallowed hard, brushing the crumbs from her jeans. This was clearly just what she needed: Wasn't it bad enough that her own mother had stolen her almost-maybe-potential-boyfriend right from under her nose, but did she really have to sit here and watch these two over-the-hill lovebirds moon all over each other in broad *daylight?*

"Antonio!" Edie trilled, holding out her cheek for Antonio to kiss as he slid into the chair beside her. "So glad you could make it."

"*Bella,*" Antonio said softly, looking over at Madison, his dark eyes the color of the ultra-decadent chocolate truffles at La Maison du Chocolat. "So good to see you again."

Even with a massive case of five-o'clock shadow obscuring his chiseled jaw and wearing a rumpled, navy velvet Gucci blazer, Antonio was still annoyingly hot. Mad rolled her eyes and looked away as Antonio took Edie's hand in his own, kissing it lightly.

"Oh my *God,*" Mad said sarcastically as Antonio pulled himself away from Edie's overly manicured paw. "Am I hallucinating? Edie, what is *he* doing here?"

"Well, I just thought that he could—" Madison cut Edie off by putting her palm in the air and raising one eyebrow in disbelief.

"Antonio?" Madison trilled sweetly. "Have you suddenly grown a vagina? Because we're supposed to be having a *girls'* day out."

Madison's sweet smile turned into a satisfied smirk as she watched Antonio's smile fade, and his face became suffused with color as he looked quickly away from her gaze and over at Edie helplessly. *Don't count on it,* Madison mused smugly as she watched Edie reach for Antonio's hand again, grasping it firmly in her own, her heavily outlined eyes widening in disbelief.

"Just ignore her," Edie said smoothly to Antonio, smiling

widely as if a million-watt bulb had just been switched on in her brain. "Madison gets positively *insufferable* around the holidays."

"It's not the holidays, *Mom*," Madison snapped, pulling her phone from her Cesare Paciotti black calfskin bag and checking for missed calls—if only to distract herself from the overwhelming sense of annoyance and anger that was making her blood boil like a steaming Jacuzzi. "It's the fact that you thought it was *appropriate* to invite Ricky Martin here to the one family tradition we have *left*."

"Look, *cara*." Antonio turned back to Madison and stared at her, his expression neutral as Switzerland. "I do not mean to cause any problems between you both, and I certainly do not wish to be where I'm clearly unwanted." Antonio stood up, pulling a pair of black Gucci aviators over his eyes.

"At least he can take a hint," Madison muttered under her breath as she drained the rest of her tea, making a face as it was now ice-cold. As Antonio turned around to leave, Edie jumped from her seat and grabbed onto his arm. Madison's mouth fell open as she watched Edie hanging on Antonio's arm like a three-year-old in a bakery begging for more bon-bons. *Desperate much?* Mad thought disgustedly as she rolled her green eyes and popped another heavily frosted petit four into her mouth. God, it was bad enough that Antonio was about a million years younger than her cradle-robbing mother, but did she have to make such an embarrassing spectacle of herself in public? Not to mention on *camera*?

"Antonio, darling," Edie said, reaching up and twining her

arms around his neck, "You simply *must* stay for a while. I won't take no for an answer!" Madison watched in horror as Antonio smiled down at Edie then bent his lips to hers, brushing them lightly. When their lips broke apart, they stood there gazing into each other's eyes like they were hypnotized. *Am I still here?* Mad thought in disbelief, her mouth falling open. She watched as Edie led Antonio back to the table and sat down next to him, reaching for the silver tray and popping a hunk of cake into his mouth while they cooed nonsensically at each other like a pair of demented, designer-clad lovebirds.

Madison crossed her arms over her C-cups and concentrated on staring at the brightly decorated Christmas tree instead of the slobbering make-out zombies in front of her. How much crap was she going to have to take before the humiliating fiasco that was her mother's love life blew up in Edie's face again? Ever since the divorce, her mother's "relationships"— if you could even call them that—seemed to end as quickly as they'd begun, often with tears and empty bottles of Cristal strewn all over the lavish baroque splendor of the Macallisters' penthouse apartment. Christmas, which had always been Madison's favorite holiday, was definitely cancelled this year. Without her father it just seemed pointless. She hoped against hope that he might agree to stop by on Christmas Day—just for a few hours. But any expectations she'd previously entertained had been ripped away like discarded wrapping paper after his secretary informed her that "Mr. Macallister is planning a sailing trip to the South of France over the holidays, and won't be back until the New Year." *Probably with some nineteen-year-old* Penthouse *pet,* Madison fumed, brushing crumbs from her lap. Besides, even if she *were* bursting with Christmas cheer, what would she and Edie do anyway? Bake cookies and sing carols? Not likely. *Screw the Christmas spirit.* Madison glowered as Antonio looked over, shooting a weak smile in her direction.

"Your mother has invited me to spend the holidays with you both—and I have accepted," Antonio said carefully, wiping the crumbs from his full lips with a white linen napkin.

"Great. I'll alert the media," Madison snapped as she stood up, throwing her black cashmere military-inspired D&G coat over her shoulders, the silver buttons flashing in the light. "It'll be a miracle if you two survive past New Year's," Mad said as she pulled her arms through the sleeves, not bothering to fasten the buttons and exhaling loudly in annoyance. Not that Edie and Antonio were paying attention anyway. The minute she got up, Edie began whispering in Antonio's ear and giggling like a love-struck teenager. As she looked at them, Madison couldn't help but feel a giant wave of sadness crashing over her—a wave she hoped to God the cameras wouldn't pick up on.

"Oh, and by the way," Madison said in a tone just saccharine enough to make Edie and Antonio quit their pawing and look up blankly into Madison's sweetly smiling face. If she'd learned anything from Edie over the years it was definitely how to fake it—even when you felt like killing someone. *Especially* when you felt like killing someone. "Bah fucking humbug," she snarled, turning on one heel and marching across the glittering, ornate lobby. *After all*, she told herself, blinking back an ocean of frustrated tears from her eyes, *no one ever could accuse Madison Macallister of being a girl who didn't know how to make an exit* . . .

But even so, as she walked out of the place that represented the happiest days of her childhood and into the frigid air blowing down Fifth Avenue, Madison couldn't help wishing that she had something that even remotely approximated a real family. After all, it was one thing to lose your boyfriend to the new girl in town, but it was something else entirely when guys started dumping you for your mom! Madison bit her bottom lip as she pushed through the front doors, checking her reflection in the shiny glass. Had she lost her trademark Macalliser hotness? Was that even possible? Still, why would any guy in his right mind prefer Edie to her? There were cameras trailing her every move on a daily basis, and, in a few short weeks the show would premiere and she'd be famous—or infamous. So then why was she suddenly feeling so . . . invisible? Ugh, there was nothing like a breakup to make you feel completely insignificant—no matter who you were. She needed a Breakover—and fast. Madison stepped onto the street, pulling her phone from her bag, her finger scrolling through her call list, searching for Frederic Fekkai when her phone erupted in her hands and began buzzing shrilly.

"What?" Madison barked, walking into the street and throwing out one hand to try to hail a cab, her platinum hair whipping around her head in a sudden gust of wind.

"Hey," Drew said nervously. "Glad I caught you."

"I'm in a hurry." Mad rolled her eyes and uttered a sound that closely resembled the piercing, slightly guttural cry of an elephant being shot with a spear. "I'm trying to get a cab. But what's up?"

"I just wanted to see if we could meet up tomorrow night." Drew cleared his throat, and in the depths of that scratchy noise she could hear how down he sounded. Come to think of it, he'd been weirdly depressed and totally unDrewlike since Sophie's party—not that it was her problem anymore. "I really need to talk to someone."

"You need to talk to someone," Mad repeated tonelessly as a cab screeched to a stop right in front of her. She grabbed the door handle and fell into the backseat, breathing hard. "God, I fucking hate cabs." The driver shot her a dirty look in the rearview mirror. "No offense," Madison said, holding the phone away from her ear. "Fifty-sixth and Park," she barked at the driver. "Look, Drew, do you need to talk to 'someone' or do you need to talk to me—there is a difference, you know."

God, she sounded like such a bitch sometimes. But she couldn't seem to help herself—especially where Drew was concerned. Ever since last spring when they had sort-of-almost lost their virginity to one another, things had definitely been far from perfect between them. Not only had he immediately run off to spend the summer in Amsterdam without even saying good-bye, but he'd started flirting with the bane of her existence that was Casey McCloy—new girl and complete loser—the minute he'd stepped foot back on the island of Manhattan.

"I know," Drew said, exhaling loudly in frustration. "And I need to talk to *you*, okay?"

"Meet me tomorrow night at Space. Nine o'clock."

"Space?" Drew said with no small amount of disbelief. "You mean you're actually going to venture *below* Times Square of your own free will?" Drew scoffed playfully, referring to Madison's disdain of anything not Upper East Side, as well as the fact that Space, one of the hottest new clubs in town, was located in SoHo—as far downtown as one could possibly get without being in Chinatown . . . or Brooklyn. "Who are you?" he demanded jokingly, "and what have you done with Madison Macallister?"

"I'm not even hearing you," Madison said sweetly, staring out the window at the traffic blurring by. "Besides, if it's good enough for the cast of *Gossip Girl*, it's definitely good enough for me."

Drew chuckled, sounding more like his old self than he had in weeks. "All right—I don't usually make it a practice to descend into the inner apex of Hipdom on a school night, but I guess for you I can make an exception."

"Glad to hear it," Mad answered with a hint of her trademark sarcasm, hoping Drew could *feel* how hard she was rolling her eyes at him. After all, he *had* mentioned once that he thought they had some kind of telepathic connection . . .

Madison pushed END with one French-manicured nail before Drew could say anything else, tossing her phone back into her bag, taking a strand of platinum hair between two fingers and studying it carefully. She was definitely still pissed at Drew, that wasn't even up for discussion—but, even so, she couldn't ignore the fact that meeting him at the hottest new club in the city was the *perfect* excuse to unveil the new, improved Madison Macallister . . .

cram session

"I totally hate calculus." Sophie St. John threw her book to the floor of The Bramford's entertainment lounge and twisted her golden hair, the color of buttered honey, into a messy bun, sticking a pencil through it to secure it firmly in place. It was ridiculous—even when Sophie was a mess, she was still one of the most glamorous, fashionable girls Casey McCloy had ever seen in all of her soon-to-be seventeen years. "I can't wait to get out into the real world so I never have to do math ever again."

Casey laughed, pulling her own newly straightened yellowish blond hair into a ponytail. "I hate to break it to you, Sophs, but math isn't exactly useless in everyday life."

"Well, that's what I like to tell myself, anyway," Sophie

said with a giggle, pushing her black Gucci glasses that she didn't need—they were strictly an accessory, as Sophie's vision was perfect—higher onto the bridge of her perfectly upturned nose, and sipping greedily at her soy latte, foam covering her lips before she licked it off, quick as a cat. With her hair pulled back, glasses on, and dressed in a tiny Ralph Lauren green-and-black plaid skirt, Wolford tights, and a kelly green Hermès wool sweater, Sophie looked more like a psychotically cheerful Catholic schoolgirl than a much-envied Upper East Side A-lister. But frequent costume changes were part of Sophie's charm—and one of the things Casey liked best about the diminutive honey-haired Bramford resident. The best, or maybe worst thing, about Sophie St. John was that she rarely took herself seriously—and unfortunately, as a result, nobody else really did either . . . In reality, Sophie was titanically smart—so much so that she'd skipped the sixth grade entirely when her English teacher discovered her plowing through Jane Austen's entire oeuvre one fateful semester, hiding battered paperbacks under her desk so she could read through her classes undisturbed.

Casey looked around the lounge, taking in the enormous movie screen hanging at the front of the room, which was currently blasting VH1's exercise in nostalgia, *I Love the Eighties*, at maximum volume, the screen filled with the image of George Michael jumping around on a runway, his hands covered in Day-Glo green gloves that were beyond horrific. A stainless steel, state-of-the-art popcorn machine that, as far as Casey could tell, nobody ever used stood in the corner, and an adjacent sculpted outdoor garden was clearly visible through a long row of windows.

Just a short month ago, merely stepping into a room like this would've caused her mouth to fall open in stunned silence. Now it was just kind of . . . normal. Casey sighed, closing her history book and tossing it on the couch beside her, crossing her legs beneath her, a pair of cabled J. Crew gray cashmere ballet flats swaddling her toes in luxurious warmth. Ever since this whole reality show thing had begun, her footwear wasn't the only thing that had changed drastically. Almost overnight she'd gone from new girl and perennial social misfit to almost . . . popular.

"How could anyone have ever doubted for, like, a *millisecond* that George Michael was gay?" Sophie said, shaking her head disbelievingly at the screen, taking in the singer's perfectly feathered golden hair, tight red athletic shorts, and signature gold hoop earring. "I mean," Sophie went on, pointing at the screen, "the ball-hugging shorts alone leave no *doubt*."

Casey burst out laughing, her shoulders shaking hard beneath her gray Fair Isle cable-knit cashmere sweater, the soft wool mirroring the exact shade of her wide-set eyes.

"Apparently no one realized that Boy George was a drag queen right away either, if you can believe that," Casey pointed out after she'd composed herself, pushing her hair back from her face with one hand. "So go figure. But, you know," she added, frowning as the Wham! video flashed off, and the girls from Bananarama started belting out "Venus," "it's weird how much better all these eighties' pop stars look now—it was like the eighties were a veritable black hole of spandex, bike shorts, leg warmers, and other assorted fashion nightmares."

With her new designer wardrobe courtesy of the producers of *De-Luxe*—and the occasional forays into both Sophie's and Phoebe's overstuffed closets—her newly straightened hair, freckles that were now magically airbrushed away with Giorgio Armani foundation, along with her newfound celebrity status, Casey had succeeded in making quite the transformation herself. When she peered into the mirror these days, she barely recognized the girl staring back at her. The weird, frizzy-haired, socially inept Casey seemed to have been banished for good with a click of a remote and the whir of the camera. The only problem was that she still wasn't sure how she actually *felt* about any of it.

But whether she really wanted to come to terms with it or not, Casey couldn't help noticing that not being treated like a social outcast was definitely preferable to being terminally typecast as a gauche, Midwestern loser. But every time she caught sight of her own reflection in one of the glossy shop windows lining Fifth Avenue, she was filled with a sudden shock, a sense of complete dislocation, and an out-of-body, *Twilight Zone*–esque sensation when she realized that the smiling, sophisticated blond staring back at her was none other than, umm . . . herself. Who *was* that girl, she sometimes wondered as Meadowlark's best and brightest routinely waved at her in the hallways and IMed her late into the night.

As soon as the student population had gotten word that

Madison and Casey had been chosen for their own reality show, the invitations to the Upper East Side's most exclusive parties and events had begun flooding in with a force and regularity that made Casey feel slightly dizzy as she stood in the kitchen each night while opening the piles of thick enve- lopes that were now routinely strewn across Nanna's granite kitchen counters. But did it really mean anything when the only reason people were interested in you was because you were on some stupid TV show? Casey shifted uncomfortably on the soft couch, the thought making her squirm.

"So," Casey began, trying to change the subject and dis- tract herself from the thoughts about her shifting identity that she really didn't want to focus on, "have you talked to your . . . mom lately?" Sophie's smile faded away as the words left Casey's lips, and she looked down at her skirt and began pick- ing at a loose yellow thread, her normally open, happy face set with concentration. Six weeks ago Sophie had met her bio- logical mother, Melissa Von Norton—an infamous Holly- wood actress who'd given Sophie up for adoption when she was just an infant—at Sophie's lavish, Studio 54–themed sweet sixteen. Needless to say, they didn't exactly leave the party making plans to have sleepovers and wash each other's hair on a regular basis. The night ended with Sophie running out of her own party, leaving Melissa—not to mention the rest of the Upper East Side—standing on the street, mouths agape. Ever since that night, Sophie had refused to talk about it with anyone . . . until now.

"She's called . . . and e-mailed a few times," Sophie said

with a sulky sigh, eyes still fixated on her skirt. "But I haven't exactly been dying to talk to her." She tossed the loose thread to the floor, her sweater falling back from her wrists to reveal a series of angry-looking red cuts that marred her pale skin. Casey couldn't help staring at the jagged, diagonal markings, her gray eyes widening with questions she knew she couldn't—shouldn't—ask as Sophie quickly pulled her sleeves down and picked up her history book, making a show out of busily rifling the thick, smooth paper. *Maybe it was her cat*, Casey thought as she groped for something to say. *Yeah, right*, her inner skeptic snarled, clearly not buying her own halfhearted explanation for a second. *Her cat just happened to scratch both of her wrists? In exactly the same place? Not likely.*

"But she's your *mom*," Casey went on, unsure of where exactly she was going with any of this—only that she knew she had to keep talking or she'd be likely to blurt out something stupid and insensitive like, "What happened to your *arm?*" And that, Casey knew instinctively, would be a complete disaster. "Don't you want to try to have some kind of relationship with her?"

Sophie snorted, closing her history book again in exasperation. "Oh, right," she said, her voice dripping with sarcasm. "Like *your* relationship with your mom is so great? Where is she again anyway?"

Casey blushed hard, adjusting her silky straight hair in its ponytail. She still couldn't believe that after years of wrestling with her impossibly curly locks that went every which way with a mind of their own, that freedom could've been as simple as a trip to Elizabeth Arden—courtesy of the beauty guru that was Madison Macallister, of course.

"She's in London, working on her book. She got some big, fancy-pants grant to go to Oxford, so she'll be there all year," Casey said, running her hands over the smoothness of her ponytail. Casey looked down at her cashmere-swaddled body and wondered what her mother, Barbara, a professor of Women's Studies at Illinois State University and card-carrying feminist, would have to say about her new look—not to mention the news that her daughter was a soon-to-be reality television star. Nothing good, that was for sure.

"You're playing right into the hands of the patriarchy—not to mention supporting the most abominable aspects of American consumerism!" Barbara would probably yell, slapping her hand down onto the battered wooden kitchen table for added emphasis. Barbara was big on punctuating her declarative sentences with furniture slaps or meaningful grunts—which was kind of strange considering that her mother had a Ph.D. . . . For someone with an advanced degree that took years to earn, her communication skills definitely left something to be desired.

"Well, it's definitely weird," Sophie said, giggling. "Every time she calls you hold the phone practically a mile away from your ear and roll your eyes until you hang up. She must be a nightmare."

"Yes," Casey said with a giggle, "but she means well . . ."

"Speaking of nightmares," Sophie said, pushing her glasses up onto the bridge of her nose for the millionth time and getting down to business. "What's up with you and Drew lately? It's been practically forever since I've seen you two licking each other's faces in the hallway, or force-feeding one another stupid amounts of baked goods at lunch."

Now it was Casey's turn to sigh and look at the floor, the smile fading from her rosy face, her pulse quickening at the mere mention of her almost-kind-of-not-really-even-her-boyfriend's name. The truth was that things between her and Drew were worse than ever. Since he'd inexplicably left her on the dance floor and run out of Sophie's sweet sixteen six weeks ago, they'd barely exchanged more than two words. Complicating things even further was the fact that Casey had been hanging out with Darin Hollingsworth, the skinny Emo guy with the shock of black hair who'd rescued her from total wallfloweritis once Drew cut out of the party without so much as a backward glance and left her standing there looking decidedly pathetic.

Every night Casey stared at her Swarovski-covered Verizon Venus—another gift from Pulse—for what seemed like hours, simultaneously willing it to ring while thinking hard about calling Drew, but chickening out every time. It seemed like the minute her fingertips pressed SEND, she immediately began fumbling for the END button, her heart flailing toward her mouth. Wasn't calling him kind of desperate? After all, he'd walked out on *her*—shouldn't *he* be the one to call? Casey crossed her arms across her chest stubbornly, her cheeks aflame again just thinking about the way he'd left her standing by herself on the dance floor, scanning the crowd for his lanky frame, so happy and relieved that things seemed to be okay again after the weird, tumultuous weeks that had led up to Sophie's party. Ever since Drew had begun a documentary film project about wealthy kids on the Upper East Side for his advanced cinema class at Meadowlark, he'd been paying less attention to Casey, and more and more attention to Madison—and interviewing her for the film certainly hadn't helped matters. It was so annoying—no matter how straight her hair, how cool her clothes, when it came to Drew, Casey felt like she was perennially at odds, and always, *always* making the wrong move.

"I have no idea," Casey finally managed to spit out woodenly, her voice strained. "I really haven't talked to him much. Unfortunately," she muttered, looking down at her hands and concentrating on her bitten fingernails.

"How come?" Sophie asked, pulling her legs swathed in black tights underneath her. "Did you guys have a fight or something? I ran into him in the hall yesterday and he looked like *ass.*"

"Tell me about it," Casey deadpanned, sighing loudly and hoping Sophie couldn't tell that she was lying through her teeth. With his artfully tousled dark hair and piercing blue eyes, no matter what Drew was going through, Casey had never seen him look less than utterly, stupidly, ridiculously gorgeous—even when he resembled a walking poster boy for Prozac. "It wasn't a fight . . . exactly," Casey mused, her words both jumbled and stuttering, sounding as confused as she currently felt. "We've just . . . stopped talking, I guess."

"Is it because of the terminally angsty Mr. Hollingsworth, by any chance?" Sophie asked with a smile, slurping the last of her latte and placing the empty cup down onto the stainless steel coffee table that separated the two couches from one another. "What's up with you and Fallout Boy anyway? I didn't think you guys were really a thing yet."

Casey furrowed her brow, pulling her knees up to her chest and hugging them tightly, unsure whether or not to tell Sophie the truth. For the last few weeks, she and Darin had been hanging out more and more—checking out revival film festivals of Pasolini and Godard, and meeting for coffee before school most mornings, sitting side by side at Uncommon Grounds, scribbling in their respective notebooks. Casey loved how comfortable she felt around the tall, lanky, dark-haired boy—she rarely erupted into an uncontrollable pool of sweat, or blushed and stammered in his presence. Being with Darin was like hanging out with your brother—or some other male entity you'd known for years. That being said, she, umm, wasn't exactly filled with the burning desire to rip his clothes off . . .

Just last week they'd said good-bye in front of The Bram after a late-afternoon study session. The sky was beginning to darken rapidly, as it always did in winter, the streetlights twinkling magically as they came on one by one, illuminating the white clouds that hung between them—a by-product of their warm mouths mixed with the shock of cold air. Darin looked at her, shaking his shock of shaggy dark hair from his eyes, and shifted his weight awkwardly. Casey knew that Darin wanted to kiss her, she knew that the way that you know it's going to snow right before the first flakes come tumbling out of the sky, blanketing the world in a soft white haze.

He leaned slightly forward, his lips turning up in a half-smile, and as much as Casey knew this was her cue to lean in and touch her lips to his, as much as she knew she was supposed to want to (hell, she should've been on cloud nine), she couldn't escape the overwhelming fact that it just didn't feel *right*. Casey exhaled loudly, flopping down on the couch and staring over at the huge widescreen plasma TV attached to the far wall. Maybe there was something wrong with her. Almost-seventeen-year-old girls should *want* to be kissed, right? *Just maybe not by Darin Hollingsworth,* her inner bitch added smugly.

"No, Sophie, we are most definitely not a *thing* yet. And I don't really know if we'll ever be. I like hanging out with him, but it's more like hanging out with a male version of you that grew up at CBGBs instead of Barneys," Casey said, imagining Sophie dressed up like a Ramone or, better yet, Debbie Harry. That would be a hot look for her . . . "He invited me to go to see some band in Park Slope on Friday night."

Sophie's mouth fell open. "You're going to Brooklyn? Of your own free will? For the love of God, *why?* There's nothing there but lesbian stroller moms and grimy coffeehouses where unwashed hipsters hang out and talk about their 'art.'" Sophie shuddered and began thumbing through the pages of her dreaded calculus book, shaking her head in mock disbelief while watching the page numbers she was supposed to be studying breeze by in rapid, cartoonlike succession. "Listen, Casey, if things are really over between you and Drew then, I mean, you *need* to have some new man candy on your arm. But Darin? He's not exactly the kind of guy who can make your ex jealous."

Casey felt a strange jolt in her gut as she found herself silently agreeing with Sophie—overwhelmingly so. She didn't like that jolt. It seemed wrong and totally alien. *Since when have I cared about what other people think?* Drew might be an oil painting with a cardiovascular system and a perfect ass, but Casey hadn't been attracted to him for those reasons alone— although they certainly didn't hurt. Why should she be worried about what Darin looked like or whether or not Drew was jealous?

"I'm not just trying to make Drew jealous," Casey said, not sure if it was just a teeny-tiny white lie or a completely gigantic one. "I really *like* hanging out with Darin. I just don't know if I, um, you know, *like* him."

"Your dating life is starting to sound more complicated than this damn calculus," Sophie said jokingly while throwing the math textbook into her bulging Louis Vuitton cherry-studded satchel. "You know I love you, but if this whole like-versus-like thing gets to be any more like a quadratic equation, I'm going to have to drop you like I *wish* I could drop calc." Sophie grinned as she got up and headed for the door, her bag slung over her shoulder. "Call me if you manage to figure all this 'like' stuff out. Or better yet, drop it altogether—I'll be more than happy to talk shop about boys that will undoubtedly make

Mr. Van Allen fall to his knees and start bleating your name uncontrollably like a crazed sheep."

Watching her friend walk out of the door, Casey imagined the opening credits to *De-Luxe*—how they'd introduce all the characters with short, pithy montages, summing up their fabulous lives in a few short seconds. Casey imagined how her section might be edited—quick cuts of her laughing over brioche and coffee at Uncommon Grounds, montages of her walking in the park with Sophie, her newly straightened hair blowing gaily in the wind, and shopping with Madison in some glorious Fifth Avenue boutique. And, of course, the final shot would have to be Casey standing in front of The Bram, her body leaning toward Darin's in slow motion, his lips gently touching hers, the year's first snow gently falling from the sky, coating their hair and clothes with traces of delicate white powder . . .

Wait. Rewind.

Casey closed her eyes, shaking her head vigorously in order to wipe the scene from her mind, and replay it. As the newly edited montage rolled along, she was suddenly kissing *Drew* in front of The Bram, her arms wrapped around his neck, the snow blanketing their bodies as she pulled his deliciously warm body closer still, wishing she could climb inside of him and never come up for air—or anything else—ever again.

Casey opened her eyes and frowned, more confused than ever. The choice that would be made by the producers in the editing room was obvious. It wasn't like Darin was ugly or anything—he was just . . . different. *Kind of like you used to be*, her inner bitch whispered knowingly as Casey gathered up her books from the sleek leather sofa, hugging them tightly to her chest. *But am I really going to live my life* for *this show?* Casey thought, walking toward the door and switching off the overhead lights with a snap that was more decisive than she felt. *And why was that thought suddenly so tempting,* she wondered as she swung the door shut behind her with a click.

But did she really want to give up her newfound social status to go back to being the old Casey McCloy—the girl everyone either laughed at or ignored? It was undeniable. She really, *really* hated to admit it to herself—or anyone else for that matter—but finally being on the inside was really starting to feel kind of . . . addictive.

Casey walked across the gleaming marble lobby that had begun to feel as familiar to her lately as the house she'd left back in Normal, Illinois—the white Victorian with the slightly sagging porch she'd loved to sit out on during hot summer nights—and stepped into the elevator, holding her breath as the lurching movement made her suddenly dizzy and, as the elevator climbed higher and higher still, her head fuzzy and light.

beautiful
stranger

Drew sat in a cracked red leather booth at Uncommon Grounds, a mug of inky black Colombian coffee before him as he watched the early morning sky through the plate glass window lighten to a smoky gray streaked dramatically with lavender. Drew forced himself to quit contemplating the dawn and looked down at the blank page of the spiral-bound notebook in front of him as he tried desperately to think of something to say—but, as usual, it was an exercise in futility. Maybe it was because he had a tragically hopeless case of writer's block, but just maybe, he told himself, it had more to do with the fact that it was six o'clock in the morning and he could barely read a stop sign at that hour, much less produce anything even vaguely coherent on the written page.

Drew looked around at the comforting interior of the coffee shop. The bright yellow walls and gray Formica tabletops were comforting and familiar, along with the hurried New Yorkers that surrounded him, slurping organic coffee made from freshly roasted beans, and feasting on free range–egg omelets with imported Parma ham and baby asparagus. With the SATs coming up this spring, and a course load that threatened to give him an academic hernia, now more than ever Drew needed to stay focused. He'd decided to get an early start before school to try to hack out some much-needed final interviews for *The Upper Crust*, a documentary he was making for his advanced film class, a film that would hopefully explore the lifestyles of the rich and famous—otherwise known as the crème de la crème of the Upper East Side. But lately, his work ethic seemed to consist of an endless feedback loop of the same old story. No matter how hard he wanted to write, his thoughts stubbornly crossed their arms over their metaphorical chest and refused to come out—and even when they did make it halfheartedly out onto the page it seemed like Drew was incapable of expressing himself in anything other than a jumble of nonsense. His depression was so deep and persistent that it made him feel strangely surreal most of the time, like he was walking around in someone else's life entirely.

Not helping matters much was the fact that Drew began to panic slightly every time he remembered that he had only a few short weeks before his film was scheduled to be screened in front of the entire class—and, for once, Drew found himself semi-caring whether the final result was actually any good at all, as the class was taught by none other than Paul Paxil—the enfant terrible of the indie film world and Meadowlark alum—who had returned to his alma mater this semester as a guest lecturer.

Paxil had taken Sundance by storm a few years ago with the release of *Blue Blood*, a critically acclaimed tour de force of a documentary that chronicled the life and recent murder of an infamous New York socialite. Paxil was a grade-A asshole and a certifiably pretentious lunatic, but weirdly enough, the more time Drew spent in his class, the more he found himself actually starting to respect the guy. So what if he made films about dead socialites and had a tendency to scream bloody murder every time someone walked into class carrying a Starbucks cup or dared to wear anything with a logo? Listening to Paxil's insane anticapitalist rants was definitely preferable to thinking about Drew's own messed-up life—which had fallen completely apart with a speed and velocity that left him breathless and unsure of just about everything, and more than a little terrified.

Ever since Drew had found his father in a clandestine lip-lock with Madeline Reynaud, Phoebe's mother, in a darkened corner at Sophie's sweet sixteen party, Drew felt like his whole world had been turned inside out. He'd always thought that his parents were the only couple left on the Upper East Side who were really, truly still in love with each other—not just faking it for flashbulbs and charity luncheons. Maybe Drew's life up until now had been an utterly predictable cliché only made possible by a certain kind of willful blindness. But the truth was that Drew *liked* things that way, he liked living in a protected little bubble fostered by the security of a two-parent household—two parents who loved one another desperately. But the moment Drew saw his father bend down and tenderly push Madeline Reynaud's hair from her face, that illusion— along with everything he *thought* he knew about his life— came crashing down, shattering his world into a million messy and irretrievable pieces.

It was a transformation so large that dealing with it on top of his day-to-day life as a high school teenager seemed impossible, which was why he hadn't called Casey since he walked out on her that night. He had barely thought about her, and in the few random moments he *had*, he wasn't sure what he thought about anything anymore—including his relationship, if you could call it that, with The Bram Clan's newest member. His emotions were tied up elsewhere, but where exactly that elsewhere was still remained unclear. He had thought that the film could be some sort of key, that if he succeeded in figuring it out, and managed to make the documentary into something that Paxil wouldn't immediately respond to with one of his hour-long diatribes about corporate America, that his whole life would instantly and magically switch back to normal. The white page in front of him, marked only with a trail of anxiously squiggled pen marks and a few small, beige dots of splattered coffee, told him that achieving such a result was not going to be all that easy. Until that page was filled—and the next and the next and the next—and *something* in his life began to make sense again, Casey, along with all other unnecessary complications, was out of the picture.

That doesn't exactly explain why you're meeting Madison tonight though, does it? he asked himself with a frown as he closed his notebook, leaning his elbows on the slick surface of the table as Laura Wood, a Meadowlark junior with hair so dark it resembled the wing of an impossibly glossy, frantically groomed crow, squeezed by, pushing Drew's full, steaming cup perilously close to the edge of the table. Drew reached out and caught the damp cup with one hand in the nick of time, and the hot liquid splashed over the rim and across his knuckles, the sensation pulling him out of his stupor with the shock of sudden pain. Laura turned around, an apologetic grin moving across her delicate features, her white teeth shining in the light.

"Sorry," she mouthed, her ears plugged with white earbuds, holding up one hand in greeting, then nervously pushing up her trademark black, rectangular glasses that made her dark eyes look large and mysterious. Laura was always carrying around a stack of thick biochemistry books that looked heavy enough to curve vertebrae on contact. Rumor had it that her dad was some famous scientist at M.I.T. who had discovered the gene sequence responsible for compulsive shopping. Judging by her mother's collection of almost unwearable couture gowns, it was fairly obvious where that particular sequence had first reared its Lacroix-obsessed, ugly head . . .

"Whatever," Drew mumbled, wiping up the spilled coffee

with a white paper napkin as he watched Laura walk out the door, fastening her navy pea coat with one hand as she moved. Drew balled up the paper napkin, looked around the crowded room, and sighed. Ever since he'd found out that his father was a cheating, two-timing bastard, he'd wanted to talk to Madison. No matter how bad or mixed up things had gotten between them, Drew knew that if he needed her to, she'd listen—and that strangely enough Madison Macallister was probably the only person left in his life who could understand exactly what he was going through right now. But that didn't mean he wanted to get back together with her, did it?

A loud giggle erupted from a table to his left. Drew turned to the side just in time to catch a group of Meadowlark freshmen girls who were stealing glances at him over their enormous latte cups. Drew scowled in annoyance and looked away. Working at home would definitely be a lot less distracting, but for the first time ever, home was the last place he wanted to be. Every time his dad began to hover uncertainly in the doorway of his room, Drew smiled tightly and pushed past him, walking into the kitchen, the bathroom, or out the front door—anywhere else was preferable to being caught in a confined space with his father. Drew couldn't imagine having to make small talk like nothing at all had happened. So what if his parents had an "open relationship"—whatever the hell that meant. It didn't mean Drew had to like it.

A day after the party, his mother had flown to Stockholm for a retrospective of her work—a trip that suddenly and inexplicably turned into an extensive European vacation. Drew's mother, Allegra Van Allen, was a world-renowned artist, and her huge, brightly colored abstract paintings graced the walls of some of the most exclusive museums in the world. During her infrequent and irritatingly chipper calls home, whenever Drew asked when she was coming back, his mother's voice turned decidedly vague. Icicles ran up and down his spine as she began to demur, deftly changing the subject the way she usually did when faced with a subject she wanted to avoid.

"Drew, honey, I've had an absolute epiphany! I'm getting the most *fabulous* ideas for my next series over here," she gushed, pausing breathlessly to gulp at the glass of Bordeaux Drew knew was clutched in her hand. The line was eerily clear—Drew could hear the sound of her swallowing, the workings of her throat as she drank the ruby red liquid, then the clinking of crystal on a bedside table as she placed her glass down. "Maybe I'll go over to Paris for a week or so after this, just to see what kind of monkey scrawl is passing for art in France these days . . ."

As she rattled on, Drew could almost see his mother's long, tanned fingers waving in the air, punctuating her sentences the way they always did when she was excited or nervous. In any case, by the time Drew hung up it was obvious that it was just going to be him and his dad for a while longer at least—rattling around their huge-ass apartment, trying not to bump each other the wrong way . . . and failing miserably.

And speaking of bumping, Drew jumped as an elbow suddenly knocked his shoulder from behind, sending his arm flying forward and his cup falling to the floor where it shattered, coffee sloshing everywhere. "Goddammit," Drew muttered under his breath as he bent down and began to pick up the shattered, jagged pieces of porcelain from the wet tile, trying to block out the muffled giggles coming from the freshman table to his left. It seemed like everything in his immediate vicinity lately—from families to cheap cups—was totally incapable of remaining in one piece.

But Drew's annoyance rapidly disappeared as he found himself looking into a pair of eyes so deeply, enormously blue that they appeared almost violet. A girl stood there in front of him biting her full bottom lip, which was rosy and pink—but in an unglossed, natural way. Her dark hair fell almost to her waist, setting off her creamy skin and sharply arched brows, her violet eyes full of apologies.

"Oh my God," the girl said, awkwardly shifting her weight from one booted foot to the other. "I'm such a klutz." She pointed shyly at Drew's shattered cup, a tentative smile hovering at her lips. "Can I maybe buy you another?" Drew felt his anger melting away into horniness as he stared at her, taking in everything from the glossy leather of her brown riding boots, which were tucked into faded jeans, up to her chocolate brown, short leather trench that tied snugly around her narrow waist.

"Sure," Drew said when he could finally speak, his face breaking into a grin—the first he'd even remotely attempted in weeks, his face stiff and unused to the stretching sensation of his flesh. "But only if you agree to sit down," Drew deadpanned. "It'll be safer that way." The girl laughed, her impossibly pink lips parting to display rows of straight, white teeth as she slid into the red leather booth across from him.

"I'm Olivia Johannson," she said, smiling shyly, her face flushed. Her skin reminded him of the roses he'd seen at the botanical gardens last year—their fragrant satiny petals were the exact shade of Olivia's perfectly pink cheeks. "Terminally uncoordinated college freshman. And you are?" She waited expectantly as the waitress approached, an irritated expression on her tight, pinched face as she placed a new cup down in front of Drew, grumbling under her breath as she stomped off, presumably to get a mop.

"Drew Van Allen," Drew said as he reached out and took Olivia's small, soft hand in his own, wondering if his train wreck of a life was finally taking a turn for the better.

rewriting history

Phoebe wrapped a long strand of glossy, cocoa-colored hair around the tip of her gold Montblanc pen and stared out the window at the traffic blurring by in the light rain that coated the clear glass, her dark eyes darting from side to side as she followed the motion of a yellow cab streaking wetly down the street. Phoebe wrenched herself away from the window and looked down at the blank pages of her history midterm, which were spread across her desk like a thick, white fan. She wondered how she was ever going to concentrate long enough to answer even just one question about the Crimean War—much less twenty of them.

Lately, Phoebe couldn't seem to focus on the pages of anyone else's screwed-up history but her own. Jared had texted and called so many times last night that Phoebe finally let out an exasperated scream and threw the phone across the room, where it landed on the impossibly deep, round, white shag rug in the middle of her bedroom floor, the blinking screen staring at her accusingly. And, weirdly enough, the quiet that crept over her body and over the staggering stillness of her room felt somehow worse than the buzzing and ringing that had so distracted her just moments before. All she wanted was to speak to him. To press TALK and hear Jared's low voice in her ear—and she couldn't.

Ever since that awful moment Sophie had found her canoodling in that corner with Jared at Sophie's own sweet sixteen party, Sophie had barely acknowledged her existence, and for the first time ever Phoebe didn't know what to do to make up for it, or how to even remotely fix things between her and Sophie. She'd been running around behind her best friend's back and lying about it to her—to *everyone*. Wasn't it bad enough that Phoebe's own mother was having some disgusting, tacky affair with Drew's *dad*? Phoebe shuddered, closing her dark eyes briefly, the thought making her dizzy. It was totally unbelievable. And Phoebe knew that the one thing she never wanted to do was to emulate her mother, Madeline Reynaud, who, in her expert opinion, was nothing more than a cheating, home-wrecking excuse for a parent who was more concerned with shopping, facials, and her own self-gratification than she was with Phoebe and her little sister, Bijoux, who was only six and utterly destroyed by the recent turn of events.

"Where's Daddy?" Bijoux had begun shrieking every night

as Phoebe was trying to get the squirming, screaming bundle of energy that was her sister into bed. "When is Daddy coming *back*?" Bijoux yelled, smacking Phoebe on the arm angrily with a tiny hand, her small, red face on the verge of tears. Every night since her father had walked out the front door with a bulging suitcase, Phoebe had heard Bijoux across the hall, crying and snuffling herself to sleep, and the sound broke what was left of her heart in two. And now that her father had moved out for good, the Reynauds' expansive apartment in The Bram seemed to echo with a resounding silence that made Phoebe unbearably sad whenever she walked through the front door, her heels clicking on the marble floors and echoing throughout the empty apartment. With her father gone and her mother's carefully crafted façade more impenetrable than ever, Phoebe found herself feeling lonelier and more adrift than she'd ever been in her life . . .

Phoebe pulled back the sleeve of her Reyes chocolate satin shirt with a huge, silky bow at the neck, and glanced at the mother-of-pearl face of the Cartier Panther watch adorning her wrist, the gold links gleaming in the light. Her stomach growled noisily and insistently beneath her plaid wool jumper in shades of brown, cream, and burnt orange. The only time of day Phoebe usually looked forward to with excitement and relief had suddenly become almost unbearable—it was like there was an enormous pink elephant in the Dining Hall, stuffed into a tiny purple tutu, and nobody wanted to talk about it. Phoebe knew that today's lunch hour would be like every other since the party—Casey would stare at her plate and try her best to make small talk while Sophie would intermittently glare at Phoebe while shredding her salad into minuscule green slivers with the sharp tines of her fork. Even Madison, who was usually poised and unflappable, seemed both bemused and uncomfortable lately.

When she was being honest with herself, Phoebe knew that Sophie had every reason to completely hate her, but Phoebe *also* knew that she really was trying like hell to do the right thing—even if it was too little too late. It had been beyond hard to keep avoiding Jared, but breaking up with him before the party had been the right thing to do. Every time she looked into his blue eyes, or his number flashed across the screen of her phone, it had made her feel so horribly guilty she could barely stand it. Still, every time she closed her eyes, she couldn't help seeing his face, smelling the salty, citrus scent that clung to his skin that always seemed to be kissed by the summer sun—even in the blast of frigid December wind that had recently begun flying down the city streets. But no matter how badly she found herself wanting Jared with every pore of her skin, every fiber of her being, no guy was worth losing one of her best friends over. There had to be something she could do to make Sophie come around . . .

Enough is enough, she muttered under her breath, placing her pen down on the desk and grabbing her phone from her bronze Gucci hobo from the Hysteria collection, her fingers pecking out the words she'd wanted to say but been too afraid to utter out loud for over a month now.

Can we talk?

she wrote, holding her breath as she pressed SEND, her hands shaking. Phoebe waited nervously, watching as the screen remained blank. There was always the possibility that Sophie might not answer at all—it wasn't like she owed Phoebe any favors or even the courtesy of listening to her litany of apologies. The screen of her phone flashed brightly, and Phoebe's heart sped up in her chest like a motor coughing and sputtering as she looked down and read Sophie's curt reply.

About what?

Phoebe sighed, her confidence deflated. Crap. This was going to be harder than she'd thought. Not that she'd expected Sophs to welcome her back with tears and an armful of flowers as a peace offering or anything . . . Phoebe was all too aware of the fact that if anyone should've been bringing anyone a bunch of expensive, out-of-season hothouse blooms, it should've been her. Phoebe took a deep breath, tried to ignore the tension in the room and the sounds of frantic scribbling all around her, and attempted another note.

I miss you, Sophs . . . and I'm really, really sorry.

Phoebe winced slightly, exhaling as she pressed SEND. Why did telling the truth always make her feel so vulnerable? And it *was* the truth, after all. She did miss Sophie—she missed her every time she slid into her chair across from her best friend at lunch and saw the vacant stare that wiped out Sophie's delicate features, hardening her usually sunny expression into a jaded mask. She missed the way Sophie's eyes sparkled mischievously when she was excited or happy. She missed spending whole afternoons trying on crazy felt hats with feathers and Stella McCartney dresses at Barneys. But most of all, Phoebe was sorry. She was sorry she'd lied about something so important, so full of regret that she felt nauseous whenever she caught sight of her own reflection in the mirror, her pulse racing as she blinked rapidly in disbelief and looked away. Who exactly had she become? What kind of person dated her best friend's brother and lied about it?

Me, I guess, Phoebe thought miserably as tears welled up in her dark eyes. Whoever she had briefly become, Phoebe knew that she didn't want to be that manipulative, secretive girl ever again—and she was going to do whatever it took to not only make things right, but to banish that girl from her heart forever. *Please, Sophs*, she thought, closing her eyes and gripping the phone tightly in her hands, *please let me make it up to you.*

Phoebe opened her eyes just as the screen glowed brightly again, and her rapidly beating heart, buoyed by a combination of happiness and relief, jumped in her chest as she read Sophie's reply.

K. Talk 2 U later.

multiple choice

Madison gnawed obsessively on the end of her pencil, the bitter taste of graphite filling her mouth as she reached out one hand to touch her new chocolate brown locks, which fell in a dramatic sweep to her shoulders, her eyes deeply green beneath a sheaf of dark bangs that angled sharply over her left eye, while simultaneously admiring her new Christian Louboutin cognac-colored leather boots with wooden platforms that were tucked into a pair of distressed Just Cavalli jeans. It was going to take forever to grow these stupid bangs out once she was sick of them, but who cared as long as she looked fabulous right now—which, predictably, she did.

Maybe she'd even keep this look for her college interviews next year—it made her look more . . . serious in a hot,

Angelina Jolie–esque sort of way. All she needed was a private plane and a burka, and she could promptly begin importing infants from the Middle East, hiring a legion of nannies to look after them at her sprawling Upper East Side compound. *I wonder if Dior makes burkas*, Mad thought, dreamily staring into space as she pictured herself standing in front of the U.N. dressed in a black Chanel suit, one lone tear rolling down her discreetly rouged cheek as she clutched a sparkly gold medal to her chest . . .

What the hell does U.N. stand for anyway? Madison thought, wrinkling her brow and looking back down at her French midterm, silently lamenting the fact that even though she'd been in class for at least twenty minutes, the thick sheaf of papers cluttering her desk was still almost completely blank. Madison sighed heavily as she gnawed even harder on the end of her pencil, leaving deep gouges in the wood with her perfectly even white teeth. Ugh, why did she ever decide to take French in the first place? It wasn't like she was going to run off to Nice with a hot guy anytime soon, which, as far as she could tell, was the only reason the French language would prove to be even remotely useful in her life. And after the recent Antonio fiasco, truthfully she'd had enough of Euro hotness for a while. Lately, every time she walked through the front door of her apartment, she was faced with the horrifying sight of Antonio and Edie gazing into each other's eyes as they sat drinking flutes of Cristal in the Macallister's overly decorated Louis XIV–esque living room, or feeding each other bites of roasted sea bass Edie had ordered in from Babbo while making ridiculous, disgusting baby noises into each other's moony faces. Barf. It was almost enough to make her get on a plane to Dubai and put *herself* up for adoption . . .

Madison removed the pencil from between her caramel-glossed lips, leaned her elbows on the desk, and distractedly ran her hands over the arms of the Balenciaga ultramarine wool blazer with a fluffy fox fur collar Edie had brought home last week and left on her bed—no doubt as some kind of peace offering. "Dream on," Madison muttered under her breath as she picked up her pencil again and began doodling a series of ornate Chanel double-C's in the margins of her exam.

But even if there wasn't a hot Euro stud in her near future, at least she had her date with Drew tonight to look forward to. Well . . . sort of. Drew had never exactly been Mr. Sunshine in the first place, but ever since Sophie's party he had been moodier than usual, moping around Meadowlark's hallways like someone had just told him that Woody Allen, his favorite filmmaker, had finally dropped dead from chronic hypochondria.

Madison moved on from Chanel double-C's to Gucci horse bits, heavily shading a fairly large, elaborate symbol in the white space provided to answer question number five. *Ce n'est pas un Gucci handbag*, Madison thought to herself, feeling a deep desire to walk straight out of the classroom and into a cab. *Barneys, stat!* She finished the doodle, lifting the pencil to admire her handiwork, noticing that the ends of the beloved emblem looked like a pair of mirrored D's. *Très jolie*, she thought smugly, the smile fading from her face as she thought back to that awful night last spring before Drew left for the summer in Amsterdam.

Madison had nearly worn a Gucci dress on that unenchanted balmy spring evening—the night of their ill-fated attempt at losing their respective virginities. Afterwards, she'd briefly obsessed as to whether things would have gone better— gone anywhere except to the bathroom to puke—if she hadn't made that last-minute change. She hated when she even remotely entertained thoughts like that—it was beyond ridiculous to think that the wrong choice of clothing could alter the course of your entire sexual destiny. *Superstitions are for Birkenstock-wearing, granola-eating Upper West Siders,* Madison thought, sneaking a peek at Drew, who was sitting to her left and was presently bent over his midterm, scribbling furiously as his dark hair flopped, as always, into his blue eyes. *How the hell can he even see,* she wondered, shaking her head in amusement, *much less answer these ridiculous fucking questions?*

While only a matter of months had passed since that embarrassment of a date, it seemed like an eternity ago—a feeling that was easily justified by the amount of French she had obviously failed to learn. She had started and ended a career as a model and was shooting her first reality TV show—her life was so totally different now that she might as well have had a baby, moved to London, and converted to Judaism. *Maybe that's not such a bad idea—Jewish moms are so hot right now . . .* However, she drew the fucking line at studying Kabbalah. Maybe she'd get one of those red string bracelets all the celebrities were wearing lately and just call it a day . . . But no matter how things had changed in the world of Madison Macallister, Drew, apparently, had remained the same. Well, not completely the same—there was the whole Casey nightmare, not to mention his recent dark-and-tortured-soul stage. Maybe the new Madison—brunette, former model and soon-to-be reality TV star extraordinaire—could achieve what the old Madison, as fabulous as she was, could not.

Madison shifted in her seat, crossing her legs encased in tight denim, a strange, tingly sensation spreading through her limbs. Instead of being annoyed by Drew's girly moodiness the way she normally would've been at any other moment, for some reason it struck her as kind of . . . hot. Or maybe she just needed to lose the technicality that was her virginity before her vagina became as obsolete as pay phones on Manhattan street corners. *Or,* her inner pragmatist whispered bitchily, *maybe you're only interested in what you don't have, and, until Ms. Annoyingly Normal got her claws into him, didn't want.*

"Touché," Madison whispered under her breath, a smile turning up the corners of her lips, delighted at her own witticisms. Her inner monologues were so amusing, she sometimes wished she could broadcast them to the entire class. Madison shifted in her chair, crossing her left leg over her right and throwing her mass of newly darkened hair over one shoulder. Whatever was going on in the depths of her Cavalli jeans, maybe tonight she could kill two birds with one stone—get Drew back AND enter the realm of womanhood. Dammit, it wasn't *fair.* If *any- one* deserved a virginity do-over, she did . . .

Madison bit her bottom lip in exasperation as she finally gave in and scribbled her name across the top of the page in large, looping letters, weighing her options as her pencil scratched the slick paper. If she *did* actually get back together with Drew the way she'd been planning, she could finally take care of that annoying Casey problem once and for all—with the added bonus of creating excellent television in the process—not that she really needed much of a *reason* to manufacture drama and chaos in other people's lives.

Besides, she told herself as she began rapidly filling in the answers, her script scrawling across the white pages, her knuckles smudging her words as she wrote, *bringing le drama is its own reward* . . .

make up and
make out

Sophie crossed her legs covered in Juicy olive cashmere sweatpants beneath her, shifting uncomfortably in the silence that hung between her and Phoebe, who was perched on the edge of the bed like she might bolt at any moment. The tension between them was so thick it might as well have been made of silicone. It was weird—Sophie usually considered her bedroom to be the place where she felt more comfortable and secure than anywhere else in the world. Everything from the bright purple walls and ultramod white plastic and resin accessories to the giant, slightly dilapidated golden brown teddy bear propped in the corner with the red bowtie that her father had won her at South Street Seaport when she was nine screamed of safety and home. The trouble was ever since she'd found out she was adopted, it was hard for Sophie to think of anyplace as home anymore—everything she had previously thought was hers now belonged to someone else's life, including her friends.

Sophie watched as Phoebe took a deep breath, her chest beneath the chocolate satin shirt she wore expanding as the air rapidly moved into her lungs. "Sophs," she began, looking up, her dark eyes welling with tears as they met Sophie's level gaze. "I don't know what to say. I screwed up. Big-time. I don't know how I can make it up to you. But I really, really want to try." Phoebe's eyes shone with unshed tears, and she looked away, sniffing loudly.

Sophie exhaled, pulling her mass of hair down from where it rested in a messy bun at the back of her neck, and combing through it with her fingers distractedly as she watched Phoebe look away, clearing her throat with the guttural scraping noise she always made when she was about to collapse into tears. If the cameras were there, maybe things would be different— maybe Sophie would find herself magnanimously forgiving her best friend, and folding her into her arms for a hug, one eye tearfully fixed on the lens as the shot faded out into a slow dissolve to black. But Sophie didn't feel like hugging anyone—on or off camera. In fact, the trouble was that she wasn't really sure she knew how she felt about anything anymore, including Phoebe and Jared.

"Sophs," Phoebe said quietly, picking at the comforter with one hand while looking away, "I never meant to do anything to hurt you. I wanted to tell you so many times but I just . . . couldn't." Phoebe shrugged her delicate shoulder. "I don't know why. I guess I thought you'd be . . . mad."

"You guessed right," Sophie snapped, pulling her knees to her chest and hugging them tightly with her arms. Maybe if she pulled herself into a tight enough ball, she'd start to feel safe again. Then again, if she pulled far enough into herself, maybe she'd just disappear altogether. Sophie watched as the tears started to slide down Phoebe's cheeks, her nose running wetly as she cried. It was ridiculous, even when she was all wet and snotty, Phoebe looked like she should've been somewhere insanely glamorous—like Maldives, sipping a tall, rose-colored cocktail under an umbrella, wearing a white Yves Saint Laurent one-piece as she ordered her cabana boy to push her chair farther into the sunlight with a snap of her long fingers.

Sophie sighed, letting go of her knees and crossing her legs beneath her again, as she pulled her olive cashmere hoodie around her body, checking to make sure it was covering the red cuts on her wrists that just wouldn't seem to heal, no matter how much Neosporin she slathered on the scabs. She'd slipped up lately—there was no denying it. *This is the last time*, she'd told herself just last week, as she turned the lock on her bathroom door and slid down to the floor, popping the sharp blade from the bright pink confines of a disposable razor. It was a momentary loss of control, her therapist, Dr. Breuer, explained the next day in tones so soothing her voice made Sophie want to lie down on the plush emerald-green-and-tan Persian rug covering the polished parquet of her office and take a big nap.

"But that doesn't mean it has to start all over again." Dr. Breuer peered carefully at Sophie over her red Alain Mikli frames. "You always have a choice, Sophie—it's up to you."

Sophie knew that Dr. Breuer was right—it wasn't like she *couldn't* stop herself if she wanted to. The problem was that sometimes she just didn't *want* to.

And Sophie knew that everything wasn't entirely Phoebe's fault. After all, it wasn't as if she'd exactly been easy to talk to lately, or even *available*. But with everything that had happened, who could really blame her? Finding out you were adopted, meeting your biological mother, and turning sixteen would be a lot to handle under the *best* of circumstances, and simultaneously feeling betrayed by one of her closest friends certainly hadn't helped things either.

Maybe it was all just a case of bad timing, Sophie mused, watching as Phoebe caught her full lower lip between her teeth, biting down while wiping the delicate skin beneath her eyes with her fingertips. If the proverbial shit hadn't hit the fan all at once, maybe she wouldn't have taken it so hard when she found out about Phoebe and Jared. It wasn't the fact that they were obviously crazy about each other that bothered her so much, but the idea that Phoebe had lied to her and snuck around behind her back for God knows how long. It's not like Jared didn't lie, too, she told herself. But what did she really expect from a brother who only paid attention to her when he wasn't rereading old surfing magazines or sneaking around with her best friend? She'd expect this kind of betrayal from the annoying, unwashed, food-stealing presence that was her brother, but Phoebe? She'd expected more and better from someone who was supposed to be her best friend—loyalty, or, at the very least, honesty.

"I know you're sorry, Pheebs," Sophie said carefully, as her friend turned to face her, her normally smooth, unblemished face so full of regret that Sophie stopped speaking momentarily. "Just don't ever lie to me again, okay? I don't know if I'd be able to forgive you next time."

"So . . . you forgive me *this* time?" Phoebe asked hopefully, sniffling pathetically as she reached over to Sophie's bedside table and grabbed a pink tissue, blowing her nose loudly and insistently—with a honking noise that sounded more like a foghorn than the cacophony created by the tiny sloped nose of one of the Upper East Side's most beautiful girls. Sophie nodded, giggling at the familiar sound. For someone as pretty and delicate-looking as Phoebe, she could blow her nose louder than anyone Sophie had ever met. It sounded like a cross between a blaring car horn and a pissed off tugboat.

"*Sexy,*" Sophie said teasingly. "If only my brother could see you now."

"Shut up," Phoebe said with a smile, reaching over and throwing her arms around Sophie in a hug. Sophie leaned into her friend's warm body, the smell of the Nina Ricci perfume Phoebe always wore familiar and reassuring. Maybe her family life was completely fucked, but maybe her friends were the only family she really needed . . .

"Hey, adopted one," came Jared's loud voice, his big-boy

feet stomping loudly down the hallway, crushing the warm and fuzzy moment. *I certainly don't need* him *for family,* Sophie thought to herself, desperately willing him to not enter the room—which, of course, he did. The door flung open, slamming into the wall behind it and certainly causing something, somewhere to be knocked out of place. Jared wasn't truly *in* a room until he had managed to fuck something up. Boys will be boys . . . She looked up to see her brother wearing one of her bras over his head, the white lace cups covering his eyes like some strange sunglasses that Nicole Richie might wear.

"Sophs, just because you were adopted doesn't mean you can eat like one of those starving African kids—could you at least *try* to leave some milk and cereal so I can eat breakfast?" He pulled the bra off of his head and threw it toward her, about to turn and leave the room when he saw Phoebe sitting on the bed. It was all Sophie could do to not burst out laughing at the look of shock she saw on his face and the quick, short breath she heard Phoebe suck in. *And I thought that I would be the uncomfortable one.*

"It's hardly breakfast time," Sophie exclaimed, rolling her eyes at her brother's stupidity. "It's four in the afternoon—in case you didn't know."

"Whatever," Jared said coolly, his blue eyes locked on Phoebe's face. "Any time's a good time for cereal."

"Who are you, Tony the Tiger?" Sophie snapped. "Get out of my room! And if you've stretched out my La Perla, I'm going to put your ass on the next plane to Zimbabwe."

"Please?" Jared retorted sarcastically as he stood in the doorway, staring at Phoebe like a love-starved lunatic. Sophie watched as Phoebe raised her head, her eyes meeting his, a look of such pure, unabashed longing contorting her features that Sophie almost wanted to leave the room, just so they could have some privacy. Looking at the way Phoebe and Jared stared at each other like they wanted to devour one another from head to toe made it immediately and painfully clear to Sophie that you couldn't fight destiny—or love, for that matter. It was just like Shakespeare said—the heart wanted what it wanted, and nothing else was even remotely capable of appeasing it. Or something to that effect anyway . . .

"I really don't know what you see in him, Pheebs," Sophie said dryly, shaking her head from side to side in disbelief. "He's a total moron."

But Phoebe wasn't exactly listening to her, or to anyone. Her eyes were locked on Jared's, a slow, dreamy smile creeping over her face as if she was having the most delicious dream ever. The sparks between her dumbass brother and her best friend that were currently hurtling themselves across her bedroom were undeniable—in fact, they were practically phosphorescent. It was obvious that if Pheebs and Jared were meant to be together, then there wasn't much she, or anyone else for that matter, could really do about it. And just seeing the way Phoebe and Jared stared at each other, the way they were completely oblivious to anything or anyone else in the entire world—including her—made Sophie's chest ache just a little for a boyfriend to call her own.

three, two,
one . . . blast off

Drew sat at the bar at Space in a high-backed, vaguely uncomfortable white plastic chair, the melodious, calming sound of Air's Talkie Walkie CD streaming through the speakers overhead. Drew tapped one foot nervously against the floor, wondering just what the hell he was doing here in the first place. Was it possible to have a mid-life crisis at seventeen? Just this morning he had found himself feeling totally attracted to Olivia—not only had he pretended to be a freshman at Princeton, home for a "family emergency," but, before he could stop himself, he'd programmed her digits into his phone *and* asked her out for Friday night. And now, here he sat, waiting for Madison to sweep into the room and make her grand entrance. What the hell was going on with him anyway?

Drew looked around at the white, glossy floor beneath his feet, the glaring white walls and plastic mod furniture from the sixties that filled the club. In the center of the room was a transparent inflatable pool, electric blue water gently sloshing at the edges. In spite of the brightness of the décor, the lighting coming from elaborate, stainless steel chandeliers shaped like industrial objects was dim and muted, and white tea lights flickered all along the length of the white resin bar he sat at, and atop the hundred or so tables scattered across the room. The vibe was *A Clockwork Orange* meets Andy Warhol's Factory, and the icy-cold, emotionless setting wasn't helping Drew feel any more comfortable with his decision to show up in the first place.

Drew turned in his seat to face the entrance just as Madison swooped through the front door in a black dress that swirled out around her endless legs, and high-heeled shiny black boots that went clear to her knees, a long black coat thrown over her slim shoulders, a leather-and-gold cuff bracelet hugging one delicate wrist. The Pulse crew trailed behind her, the red-haired producer barking orders at the production team and looking as if she wanted to kill everyone in the immediate vicinity on sight.

Oh, that's just perfect, Drew thought, running one hand through his hair, a worried expression creasing his brow. He hadn't realized that the cameras would be there, or he never would've suggested that they meet up. But, since Pulse followed Madison's every move lately, it wasn't exactly a giant surprise either. So, if he did choose to confide in Mad the way he'd been planning, his parents' dirty little secret would be broadcast not only across the Upper East Side, but shared with an audience of millions—whether he liked it or not. *But maybe that's just what they deserve,* Drew thought as Madison caught sight of him, waving one hand in the air.

A lump the size of a ripe grapefruit formed instantaneously in his throat as he watched Madison walk across the room, marching purposefully over to him with a smile so bright it could've powered all five boroughs of Manhattan. *You're not here to get back together with Mad,* he reminded himself as he took in her newly dark hair that made her eyes sparkle in the dim lighting even from a distance. *You just need a friend.* The truth was, he'd never felt so lost in his entire life, and the only constant in his life right now, whether he liked it or not, was Mad—whether they loved or hated each other, were fighting or attached to each other's mouths with some kind of invisible suction, for the last two years of his life, she had always been *there.*

"Hey, stranger," Mad said breezily as she came up behind him, placing her hands on his shoulders and leaning in to kiss Drew on one cheek, bringing the scent of cold wind and a slight hint of snow into the room with her—not to mention simultaneously flooding his senses with the familiar scent of the jasmine-infused Frédéric Malle perfume he knew she only wore on special occasions.

"Hey yourself," Drew said, determined to keep things light, no matter how awful he felt about his disaster of a life.

"Been waiting long?" she asked, sliding onto a chair and

crossing one long leg over the other. Drew willed himself not to look as her dress fell away from her body, exposing one bare thigh.

"Yeah," Drew admitted, smiling as he motioned to his own glass, silently alerting the bartender to bring Madison a Manhattan. "But it was worth it." *What are you doing?* his inner dating cop shrieked silently. *Stop flirting with her!*

"So, what's this all about anyway?" she asked, turning to face him. In that one movement as her body turned toward his own, Drew was struck, as always, by how perfectly beautiful Madison really was. It was unbelievable. In the two years he'd known her, he'd never seen her looking less than jaw-droppingly perfect. It was almost frightening.

"Some stuff has happened, and I just thought we could talk," Drew began, hating the sound of his own unsure and muddled voice. Why was talking about your feelings so horribly difficult? Not to mention awkward. Suddenly, the thought of having to explain his fucked-up family drama in detail made him want to run screaming out the front door of the club and directly into traffic. Drew took a deep breath and a swig of his Manhattan for courage, and soldiered on. "I found out the night of Sophie's party that my dad's been having an affair."

"What?" A shocked expression replaced the smile Mad had been wearing just seconds before the words fell from his lips. "Since *when?*"

"I don't really know," Drew said glumly, toying with the red plastic stirrer in his glass. Mad angled her body closer, placing one hand on his arm, her touch utterly distracting him. Drew could feel the heat from her warm body radiating through the navy blue Lacoste sweater he wore, seeping into his very skin. *Concentrate*, he told himself. "But that's not the worst part."

"It's not?" Mad asked, a bemused expression replacing the shock on her face. "Uh . . . no offense, but what could be *worse?*"

"My dad told me that they have some kind of arrangement," Drew said, practically spitting the words from his lips just to get them out of his mouth. "Apparently, my mother knows all about it."

"You mean like an open marriage or something?" Madison frowned, her smooth forehead scrunching into a mass of horizontal lines. "Didn't those go out of style in the seventies?"

Drew laughed sharply, his breath catching in his throat as he sternly ordered himself not to even *think* about crying in front of Madison—or on camera. "I guess so," Drew said, kicking one blue Puma against the bar. Maybe if he kicked himself hard enough, he'd stop wanting to push Madison's dress all the way up and run his hands over the satiny skin of her thighs. It was amazing how he could be totally depressed one moment, and thinking about throwing a girl to the floor and climbing on top of her the next.

"Are you . . . okay about all this?" Mad asked tentatively, increasing the pressure of her hand on his arm and squeezing lightly. Her eyes were so deeply green beneath her newly darkened hair.

"Do I *look* okay?" Drew snapped, pulling his arm away in annoyance. One thing he didn't miss was Madison's stupid questions—not to mention her complete and utter lack of tact.

"Not really," Mad said dryly as the bartender placed her Manhattan down in front of her, the ice tinkling softly in the glass. Drew watched as she fished out the cherry with her long, tapered fingers, and popped the round, red fruit in her mouth. "But you always kind of look like this so it's hard to tell. Who the hell is your dad sleeping with anyway? I know everyone you know, and I can't imagine your dad sticking it in *any* of them."

"Nice," Drew said, his face cracking into a smile despite the fact that he suddenly wanted to strangle Mad more than he wanted to climb on top of her. "I don't know if I should tell you."

Now it was Mad's turn to be annoyed. She rolled her eyes and raised one sharply etched, newly darkened brow. "Oh yeah? I get all dressed up and drag my ass all the way down here to meet you on a *school night* and you really think you're going to hold out on me? I don't think so."

"Ha." Drew laughed, draining the last of his drink and signaling for a refill. "Since when does the fact that it's a school night mean *anything* to you?"

"Good point," Mad said soberly as she took a dainty sip of her drink, grimacing as the liquor hit her throat. "God, Drew, why the hell do you drink these things? They taste like battery acid and gasoline."

"What does it matter *who* he's sleeping with anyway? I didn't ask you down here to gossip, Mad. Isn't the very idea of my parents having an open marriage and sleeping with God knows who—well, I *know* who, but again, that's besides the point—enough cause for concern? I mean, I could really use, you know, a friend right now."

Mad laughed out loud, picking up her drink and throwing at least half of it down the back of her throat, despite how hideous she found it to be. "A *friend?*" Madison nearly shouted. "Drew, I know this sucks and all, but if by a friend you mean someone that has gone through the same thing, who can tell you that, yeah, it's bad, but it's going to be okay, you called the wrong girl. Your family is like the Brady Bunch minus, uh, a whole *lot* of people compared to my family." Mad tossed her hair back defiantly as the camera moved in for a closeup. "I may not know exactly who your dad is sleeping with, but I know that it's not me and I highly doubt it's Casey, so with all of your exes and recent love interests off the list, you can't even *begin* to compare this small storm to the tsunami that is *my* home life."

"Oh yeah?" Drew answered back, one eyebrow raised in disbelief. "My mom's in Amsterdam right now, using the whole trip as an excuse to feed her creative genius or something, when we all *know* it's just so she doesn't have to deal with my father."

"*My* mom's whacked out on Valium twenty-four-seven," Madison snapped, "and she's currently dating some Italian guy young enough to be her son. Oh—and did I mention that he just *happens* *to* be the last guy I was even *remotely* interested in?"

Drew bit his bottom lip in order to keep a straight face and looked away, staring into the bottom of his empty glass. "Wow. That's pretty bad," he managed to blurt out before he collapsed into giggles, leaning over the bar and laughing until his entire torso ached, and he had to hold onto his sides with both hands. Mad joined in, the two of them grabbing each other and holding on for support, their hilarity building to a fever pitch that bordered on slightly uncontrollable. This was one of the things Drew had always loved about Madison— she might be bitchier than a drag queen on a bad hair day, but they undoubtedly shared not only some of the same history, but the same sense of humor as well. Mad could always make him laugh when no one else had a shot in hell of getting him to crack so much as a smile.

"Oh my God," Madison managed to blurt out as she leaned back, wiping her eyes with a white napkin. "My stomach hurts from laughing." Drew looked at the way Madison's cheeks were flushed, at the blood moving beneath her smooth, perfect skin, at the light glinting off her chestnut-colored hair, and he wanted, more than anything at that moment, to be close to her, to feel his hands on her skin, her mouth moving under his. *Don't move,* he told himself sternly as she stopped laughing, holding his eyes with her own level gaze, her expression suddenly serious and pensive. *Don't breathe. And above all, don't even fucking* think *of kissing her.*

Madison moved closer, resting her hand on his arm again

for support. She was so close that he could smell not only her perfume, which enveloped him like a net, but her skin itself—a scent that reminded him of freshly bloomed, rain-soaked lilacs. Before he knew quite what was happening, she had leaned into him, her rosebud lips touching his softly, then more insistently as their kiss grew longer, her mouth opening beneath his, her tongue drawing lazy circles in his mouth. Drew closed his eyes and melted into the sensation, wondering just what was happening to the Drew Van Allen who always had it all together. What was he doing? Last month he was with Casey, this morning Olivia, and now Madison's tongue was in his mouth—and he wasn't exactly beating her off with a stick either. The cameras pushed in, silently recording the moment unfolding between them.

Oblivious to anything other than the feel of Madison in his arms, Drew pulled her even closer—a little more roughly this time, loving the soft little murmur of surprise she made at his boldness. As he kissed her over and over again, he couldn't help wondering if his father had been right after all—maybe he *was* too young to get serious with just one girl. After all, there was a whole city out there . . .

Drew sunk his hands into Madison's cascade of shiny dark hair, his father's recent advice ringing in his ears: "You're a young guy, Drew. You should be playing the field . . ."

it's only rawk and roll, but i like it

Casey and Darin stood outside Southpaw, last on a line that stretched all the way down the block—and then gently curved around the corner. It was the first time Casey had ventured away from the borough of Manhattan since moving to the city three months ago, and from what she could tell so far, Brooklyn couldn't have been more different. Park Slope was like a small village—even at nine in the evening the streets were teeming with people: harried-looking businessmen running errands, mothers pushing their babies down the street, their charges strapped into brightly colored, expensive-looking strollers, hipsters sitting outside bakeries eating black-and-white frosted cookies and cupcakes frosted in dreamy shades of rose and lavender, lesbian couples perusing the aisles at the

Park Slope Food Coop, wholly engrossed in inspecting the scarily fresh-looking organic fruits and vegetables.

Casey looked around the busy streets, marveling at the way this neighborhood made her feel like she was part of something in a way the Upper East Side did not. Back at The Bram, Casey always felt like she had her nose pressed against some thin, transparent window that separated her from everyone else who clearly belonged there. Even though she was almost popular now, it didn't mean she was any more comfortable with any of it. Fitting in around here seemed somehow easier—or maybe things always looked that way when you were an outsider.

"Have you ever seen M-83 live?" Darin asked, pointing to the yellow and white posters of the band they were waiting to see that lined the outside brick wall of the club.

"No," Casey answered, looking down at her battered blue Converse high-tops, glad she'd pulled them out from the bottom of her closet, as they seemed to be de rigueur for Park Slope. "But I've heard their CD," Casey said, hoping her breath didn't still smell like the falafel she'd eaten for dinner. Oh well, it wasn't like Darin had just sat there watching her eat. He'd had one, too—with extra hummus.

"You've never had a falafel?" Darin had exclaimed in disbelief when they'd passed the brightly lit, cheerful restaurant with its bloodred walls and yellow hanging lanterns.

"Darin," Casey had to remind him, "I'm from a suburb in Illinois, remember? We get our movies like six months after you do. Forget about falafels." And the falafel had turned out to be one of the best things she'd ever put in her mouth—the pita soft and doughy, the fried balls of chickpeas inside crisp on the outside and almost creamy when you bit into them. Of course, they weren't exactly the most graceful sandwiches to try to consume on a date, but somehow when her falafel fell apart on her, and her cheeks were streaked with traces of tahini, she didn't freak out the way she usually did—like the time she went with Drew to Shake Shack for burgers, and could barely choke down more than a few bites in fear that the messy sandwich would fall apart on her at any moment, making her look like a more uncoordinated loser than Drew probably already thought she was. But tonight, she couldn't have cared less. Maybe it was because she felt so comfortable around Darin, or maybe it was because she was starting to care less and less what people actually thought of her . . .

"If you walked all the way down that street over there"— Darin pointed with one arm, shaking his shaggy mop of black hair from his eyes—"you'd be in Williamsburg. Ever been there?"

"No," Casey said, nodding her head and craning her neck over the crowd to follow his finger. "Isn't that where all the people who are too cool to talk to me hang out?" she asked with a grin, looping her thumbs in the front pockets of the Miss Sixty skinny jeans she'd borrowed from Sophie last week.

Darin laughed, reaching down and gently touching Casey's hand through her belt loop, then pulled it into his own, their fingers entwining. Casey felt a rush of blood to her face, and she knew that no matter how skillful she might've gotten with the cream-colored Armani foundation that smoothed out her skin tone and erased her freckles, there were two bright circles of red burning high up on the apples of her cheeks. *If I'm not interested in Darin* that *way,* Casey thought as he squeezed her hand more tightly, *then why am I blushing like this? And why is my hand sweating all over his hand? Gross.*

"Do I seem too cool to talk to you?" Darin asked, a wry grin lighting up his angular face, his cheekbones so sharp that Casey could almost imagine herself strapping on a pair of ice skates and skating across the planes of his face.

Casey looked over at the vintage Sex Pistols T-shirt he wore beneath a black velvet slim-fitting blazer, her gray eyes scanning his skinny black jeans and the dirty black Converse sneakers on his feet. "Yes," she said soberly. "You kind of *do.*"

Darin laughed again, letting go of her now damp hand and surreptitiously wiping his palm on the leg of his jeans. *Why do I have to* sweat *so much,* Casey lamented inwardly. *I should get Botox in my palms or something . . .*

"Well, obviously I'm not," Darin answered as he reached down and grabbed hold of her hand again, clutching it firmly in his own. *My hands should come with a warning label,* Casey thought, suppressing a giggle. *Hold at your own risk.* "I've got some friends who live over there. There's a Domino sugar factory that's pretty much abandoned at night—it's perfect for skateboarding." The line lurched forward, severing their hands in the sudden rush of movement.

"It sounds like you spend more time over here than you do

in our neighborhood," Casey mused aloud, craning her neck in an effort to try to see the front entrance, which was still hopelessly clogged.

Darin shook his hair from his eyes again and shoved both hands into his front pockets. "I don't know," he began with a sigh. "I just feel more comfortable down here. Back in our hood, I'm Darin Hollingsworth, heir to the Hollingsworth's publishing empire—whatever the hell *that* means. But here I'm just Darin, who likes to skateboard and hang out, you know? It's easier—which is probably why I spend so much time on the train every day."

"I kind of know what you mean," Casey said, carefully weighing her words as she spoke. "I'm not the heir to a publishing magnate or anything, but things have really changed for me since I moved here." Casey ran one hand through her hair, shocked as always by the absence of her familiar springy curls that steadfastly refused to submit to the tyranny of brushes and combs. "Sometimes all I can think about is going back home, where everything was definitely more boring— but a whole lot simpler, too."

"That's why I can't wait to get the hell out of here at the end of next year," Darin said excitedly, his blue eyes lighting up. "What I *really* want to do is take a year off after graduation and just . . . be. Travel around the world and see everything. I am so fucking sick of doing what's expected of me— even though I find ways to get out of it most of the time anyway . . ."

A pang of jealousy struck Casey squarely in the chest as she listened to Darin talk, already picturing the places he might go—islands with crystal-clear waters and pristine tropical beaches, the Eiffel Tower lit up and sparkling against the black sky, the canals of Venice and the Duomo in Florence— all the places she'd only read about in books, or seen on the Travel Channel when she was *supposed* to be doing her homework. As the line lurched forward again, Darin, noticing that she had suddenly gone silent, reached down and took both of her hands in his own, turning to face her.

"Maybe," he began, a shy and pensive expression moving over his angular features, "maybe you could come along . . . I mean, if you're not doing anything, that is." He shrugged his shoulders and dropped her hands as the line began moving rapidly as the bouncer at the door finally began waving people through the darkened entryway.

"Maybe," Casey said uncertainly, her stomach crowded with butterflies that swooped and dipped as she looked away, her cheeks flushing hotly once again. What was going on with her lately? One minute Darin was just a friend, and the next there was a colony of winged insects breeding in her gut—not to mention all the blushing that had gone on already throughout the evening. And it wasn't even midnight yet.

Maybe a world without Drew Van Allen wouldn't be such a bad place to live after all . . . While thousands of people crossed over the East River into Brooklyn on a daily basis and holding someone's hand was far from a one-night stand, regardless of how she might or might not feel about Darin, their one date was definitely opening up a lot of doors. The line moved forward again and they shuffled and lurched their way through the doors of the club, stepping into the dark interior, full of dim red lights and old beer signs that she had seen regularly in far less ironic settings back home. Making their way toward the stage, she saw the faces of all the hipster kids around her glowing in the dim red light. But instead of feeling like they were all too cool for school—or for her, for that matter—she began to feel that these were people that, like Darin, might give her a chance to be who she was, with or without the latest transparent Marc by Marc Jacobs handbag, straight or curly hair, or reality TV contract.

Casey smiled at Darin, who grinned happily back and gestured to the bar, then held up one palm in the air to signal that he'd be back in five. Casey watched as he walked away, his thin frame disappearing into the sea of people crowding the club. Maybe she wasn't quite ready to pack her bags and move to Brooklyn just yet, but no matter what he brought back from the bar, Casey thought that she, much like Tila Tequila, just *might* be ready to give Darin Hollingsworth a shot at love.

let's get it on

Madison Macallister stretched her arms above her adorably rumpled head, stretching like a contented kitty as she luxuriated against the butter-soft, navy blue Porthault sheets covering Drew's bed. If she could've meowed at that instant, she probably would have. It had finally happened—no champagne, no vomiting, and, most important, no distractions. *I am now a woman*, she thought as she ran her hands through her hair, which was hopelessly snarled into knots that she knew would take hours to comb out. *Someone should buy me a cake or something.* She smiled happily, snuggling more deeply into the sheets as she remembered how tenderly Drew had cupped her face between his hands, kissing her lips again and again as if he couldn't get enough of her, how close she had felt to him when he finally climbed on top of her, pressing their utterly naked bodies together in a sweaty embrace. Madison wasn't sure that she knew exactly what making love really felt like, but she had a sneaking suspicion that whatever it was, they'd definitely come pretty close.

Madison rolled over on her side, running her nails lightly up the soft skin of Drew's bare arm, unable to dim the wattage on the smile she knew was plastered all over her face. *So I'm happy,* she thought, closing her eyes momentarily in bliss. *So sue me.* She'd had one moment of panic when they'd first walked into Drew's bedroom as he'd deliberately shut the bedroom door. *This is going to be complicated,* she'd thought to herself with no small amount of dread as Drew pulled his shirt off over his head, looking at her intently, the attraction between them thick as a wall of cement. There was a charge in the air that changed things between them almost immediately as their clothes fell away, an intensity that caused her pulse to throb and her head to grow dizzier as she pulled him down, kissing him tentatively. But, weirdly enough, it had turned out to be the simplest thing in the world—and now that they'd done it, everything was suddenly crystal clear. How could she have been so completely blind for the last two years? At once, her feelings were shatteringly clear—like it or not, and sometimes she definitely didn't, she and Drew belonged together. And a certain formerly curly-haired, Midwestern loser was just going to have to get used to it . . .

Just as she was about to snuggle into the crook of his arm (who knew that boys were in possession of the *best* place to rest your head all these years?), Drew moved abruptly, sitting up and swinging his legs over the side of the bed, and rubbing his temples with his fingers. Just the sight of Drew Van Allen, wearing nothing but his boxers, his golden-tinged skin shining in the weak glow of his desk lamp, made Madison want to pull Drew's fluffy goose down comforter over their heads and start everything all over again . . .

Instead, Mad sat up, propping herself against the mahogany headboard, lost in her own daydreams. A picture-perfect future flashed before her eyes: she and Drew traveling the world together, fingers locked in a tight grip while Drew went to his museums and artsy bullshit, letting go only to buy her some fabulous purse in Rome or a couture piece in Paris. Their wedding in the Hamptons, the birth of their first child—by scheduled C-section of course, with a good plastic surgeon on hand . . . Drew with a salt-and-pepper beard and increasingly chiseled face, the corners of his jaw squaring off as the years went on, making him only more and more handsome. A face-lift for her at forty. Maybe her boobs at forty-five . . . it was all so perfect. So right.

That was until she noticed that Drew wasn't exactly sharing in her dreams of wedded bliss. He was sitting on the edge of the bed, a gloomy expression on his face as he pulled his T-shirt over his head. Without missing a beat, he rummaged on the floor for his pants, standing up and pulling them up to his waist, his eyes focused somewhere in the distance as he fastened his belt buckle, his eyes avoiding her face.

"Do you need anything?" he asked woodenly, turning to look out the window. "Are you okay?"

WTF? Madison wondered as she sat straight up, pulling the sheets even more tightly around her naked body as she leaned over and began to grope the floor for her clothes. *Was she okay? Did she need anything?* All of a sudden Drew was sounding more like a waiter at the Soho House than the guy she just gave her sort-of virginity to. *Again.* She pulled her dress over her head angrily, the material ripping slightly at the neckline. Fuck. Now she'd ruined her new favorite Miu Miu dress, too. Could this night possibly get any worse? This was all so typically vintage Drew Van Allen that she almost wanted to kick herself with the heel of her Jimmy Choo boots for not seeing it coming any sooner. Of *course* he was behaving like a moody asshole instead of a proper boyfriend—he was *Drew*, and if her past experiences had taught her anything about her former, soon to be totally ex-boyfriend, it was that he was so always likely to blow it, just when any sane and rational human being would least expect it. God, he pissed her off.

" 'Am I okay?' " Mad mimicked meanly, using a simpering baby voice. " 'Do I *need* anything?' " She swung her legs over the side of the bed and proceeded to stuff her feet into her boots, grateful for the small diversion of zippers and buckles. If she *really* had to stop and focus on what was actually happening, she knew that she might just lose it completely. "You have *got* to be kidding me, Drew."

Drew's body went absolutely still as the words left her lips.

He turned around, his face full of confusion. "Mad . . . I," he began, looking away from her penetrating green eyes again and studying the floor of his bedroom like he hadn't seen it every day for the last two years. "I can't . . ." he blurted out, gulping for air like it was suddenly being rationed, his blue eyes filled with confusion and what she could've sworn was a tinge of fear. "Look, Mad," Drew went on, swallowing hard and looking down at his bare feet, "I think this was—" Mad stared at him in horror, open-mouthed in anticipation of the awful words that she just knew were about to fall from his lips, her green eyes glittering with anger.

But before Drew could say anything else, there was a sharp rap at the door, then a squeaking sound as it swung open, revealing Drew's father, Robert Van Allen, standing in the doorway, a pensive expression on his usually jovial face. *Like father like son*, Madison thought with a wave of irritation as she scooped up her bag from the floor and swung it over her shoulder. Drew's dad slowly took in the rumpled sheets of the bed, Mad's messy post-sex hair, the knowledge of what had just been going on in the room only moments before he'd barged in slowly dawning on him.

"I, uh, didn't realize you had company, Drew," his dad said, recovering quickly with a smile that could've been genuine, or strictly pasted on in order to cover up any embarrassment he might've been feeling about the fact that not only was his son obviously sexually active, but he was getting down chez Van Allen. "I'll get out of your way—I just wanted to ask you about dinner. I thought we could go out and catch a bite—but I see you're . . . busy." His face flushed red as he gestured to the air in between Madison and Drew, then turned to leave.

"Don't worry about it," Mad snapped, jumping to her feet, her bag already slung over one shoulder, grabbing her black Dolce & Gabbana cashmere coat from where it lay in a rumpled pile on Drew's floor. "I was just *leaving.*"

Madison walked to the door and pushed past Drew's father, not even bothering to say "Excuse me," or make even the slightest attempt at politeness. Fuck politeness—*and* social graces. After all, it wasn't exactly polite for your ex-boyfriend to take what was left of your virginity, and then promptly start acting like a moody, introverted asshole. She turned around and shot Drew a look that could've withered all the plants within a ten-block radius, the pain she felt clearly visible in her face, no matter how hard she tried to mask her expression. *Dammit,* she thought as she psychically willed her eyes not to even think about producing moisture. *Why do I even still care—about any of this?* When Drew's eyes dropped to the floor again, it was clearly time to make her exit.

"Fuckfuckfuck," Mad hissed under her breath as she willed Drew to open his mouth and say something, anything, just so she wouldn't feel like such an utter fool standing there, waiting for him to speak. The seconds dragged on as Drew continued to look at his bare feet, rubbing them against the satiny grain of the wood floor. *O . . . kay,* Mad fumed, her nostrils flaring slightly.

Since there seemed to be no danger of Drew actually

opening his mouth and producing anything even vaguely meaningful, Mad turned on one stiletto heel and walked down the Van Allens' long, immaculate hallway, her shoes clacking noisily against the gleaming wooden floors, Allegra Van Allen's brightly colored abstract paintings blurring into intricately patterned kaleidoscopes that shimmered before her eyes she walked out the front door, slamming it loudly behind her.

london calling

"Are you just going to sit there and fondle that remote all night? Or are you going to tell me about your date?"

Casey muted the sound on the TV with the remote and smiled as Nanna walked into the living room, decorated in the cool blue and white hues that her grandmother loved, wearing a faded pink terry cloth bathrobe she'd probably had since the Depression. Her silky gray bob was pinned up at the back of her neck, and her softly wrinkled face was shiny with night cream, her diminutive, grandma-sized feet hidden by the most enormous, not to mention the furriest, pink slippers Casey had ever seen. *That is not a good look for her*, Casey thought while suppressing a giggle. Fashionable or not, there was no doubt that Nanna certainly looked a hell of a lot *cleaner* than Casey felt at the moment. As she pulled her hair down from a pony-tail, the smell of stale beer wafted through the air, causing her to wrinkle her nose in distaste. Ugh, there was no question about it—she definitely needed a shower before bed.

"It was . . . okay," Casey said, her voice as hesitant and confused as she felt. "Darin's really . . . nice."

Nanna sat down on the blue-and-white-striped couch, pulling a cushion from behind her and holding it in her lap, her blue eyes fixed on her granddaughter. "Nice, huh?" she said with a chuckle, retrieving her spectacles from her chest where they dangled on a pearl chain, and bringing them up to her nose. "Well," she said authoritatively, "that doesn't exactly sound like an affair to remember, now does it?"

Casey laughed, drawing her knees up underneath her and flicking the OFF button on the TV, throwing the remote down on the couch beside her. "I don't know," she said with a sigh. "Ever since this whole TV show, I've been really confused . . . about everything."

"Well, I never thought that show was such a great idea in the first place—but you wanted to do it, so . . ." Nanna's voice trailed off into the distance as she threw her bony hands help-lessly into the air.

"So, you let me?" Casey said with a grin. She loved to tease Nanna more than anything. Sometimes she thought her eighty-something-year-old grandmother had a better sense of humor than most of the student population of Meadowlark Academy. Actually, it was probably better than most of the population of New York, come to think of it.

"Of *course* I let you," Nanna answered soberly, a knowing look in her eyes. "That's what grandmothers *do*—haven't you heard? We spoil you rotten." She waved one hand exasperatedly in the air, signaling that she was bored with this subject already. "But whatever happened to that Drew character anyway? Did you finally give him the boot?"

Casey's smile rapidly disappeared at the mention of Drew's name. How was she supposed to really get over him if everyone kept bringing the topic up every five minutes? "That's over," Casey said darkly, her gray eyes the color of storm clouds. "I *think.*" Nanna frowned so hard that the lines in her forehead resembled the pleats of an accordion. "I'm pretty sure," Casey added in a rush, trying to sound more confident about the whole thing.

"It sure doesn't sound like you're sure," Nanna said mildly, reaching over to the bleached pine coffee table for the ceramic bowl of Italian chocolates wrapped in shiny gold foil that she kept in the center of the table. Nanna didn't seem to eat much real food anymore—nothing that constituted actual nutrition anyway—but she had a serious sweet tooth, and it had become routine for Casey to discover ten or twelve metallic wrappers strewn around the living room in the early morning. "So what's wrong with this Darin character anyway?"

"Nothing's *wrong* with him," Casey said, frustrated that this was turning out to be more difficult to explain than she'd originally anticipated. "He's just not . . ." Her voice trailed off as she fell silent, biting her bottom lip as she tried to figure out the best way to explain how she felt, and came up totally blank.

"Drew?" Nanna finished, her blue eyes softening. "Well," she added lightly, "you can't really *expect* him to be, now can you?"

"It's not just that," Casey said, squirming uncomfortably. "I didn't think that I *liked* Darin, you know, *that way* or anything. And then tonight . . ."

"Aha!" Nanna interrupted, a wicked grin spreading over her face as she rubbed her grandmotherly hands together, relishing the drama. "You *did*."

"I got butterflies," Casey blurted out, grabbing an overstuffed pillow off the end of the couch and hugging it to her chest. "I never get butterflies unless I really like someone. And tonight, while we were waiting in line to see the show, I felt them." Casey exhaled loudly, puffing her cheeks out. "And now I don't know what to do."

"So you have two suitors," Nanna said, shrugging her shoulders and making light of the situation as usual. "So what's wrong with that? I say enjoy it while it lasts," she added with a chuckle, peering at Casey over the top of her glasses.

"It's not just that," Casey admitted. "This whole TV show thing is totally bizarre. All of a sudden people want to be my friend. I mean, it's nice not to be a social leper anymore, but if people only like me because I'm going to be on TV, or because I'm popular, then what's it really mean, you know?" Casey stopped, out of breath now and more confused than ever. "I *know* I'm still the same person underneath," she went on, muttering under her breath, wondering as the words left her lips if they were really all that true anymore.

"Oh, you worry too much," Nanna scoffed, unwrapping another chocolate. "All this stuff you're dealing with now, it's nothing—just wait until you're my age and they send you to the doctor every week. Now *that's* when you can really start to worry." Nanna gave a quick, short laugh, deftly throwing the now-naked chocolate into the back of her throat. "And so what if you pick up a leech or two—if they're around for long, their true colors will come out. You've got a good head on your shoulders—your mother made sure of that—I'm sure that you'll figure it all out."

Just as Casey was about to say something decidedly less than flattering about her globe-trotting mother, Nanna's phone rang shrilly, the sound cutting through the quiet hum of their conversation.

"It's after midnight," Nanna said crankily as she shuffled toward the phone, grabbing the handset from the cradle and barking into the receiver. "Who died?"

Casey laughed, twisting her stinky hair back up into a pony-tail to get the smell away from her face, the darkness of her mood lightened. No matter how bad things got, talking with Nanna always made her feel better. Casey flipped back on the TV and channel surfed, stopping on a cooking show on the Food Network featuring what looked like a complicated cooking demonstration of sautéing a piece of juicy-looking veal—from an animal that Casey knew was probably raised in a horrible, tiny crate—with thin slices of shockingly yellow lemon, in a pan frothing with butter. Casey felt her eyes slipping shut, as Nanna's voice, the lulling sound of the television, and the fact that she had to be up in seven hours all conspired to make her eyelids feel heavy as the manhole covers on Fifth Avenue. Just as she felt herself drifting off to sleep, Nanna's voice cut through the dream she was almost having. She was in a darkened movie theater, an obscure French film scrolling across the screen, Drew's lips touching her own, her hand in his, the weight of his delicious—

"Casey!" Suddenly Nanna was standing above her, shaking the phone in her face. "Your mother wants to talk to you."

Casey rubbed her eyes and grabbed the phone from Nanna's grasp, yawning loudly into the receiver before she spoke. "Hello?"

"Casey Anne McCloy," her mother, Barbara, began, her tone even more clipped than usual due to the totally annoying British accent she'd recently adopted. Casey winced. Whenever her mother made it a point to use her full name in a sentence, Casey knew she was probably in for it. "What's this utter nonsense I hear about you being on a television show?"

Casey's stomach plummeted to her blue Converse high-tops. She knew that Barbara, who made it a habit to embark on several militant feminist, anticapitalist rants several times a day at least, wouldn't exactly be happy to discover that her only daughter was in the process of becoming a reality TV star, but she hadn't anticipated this level of anger either, which bordered on nuclear. "Mom," she began, in a tone she hoped was placating, "it was a really good opportunity and I thought you'd—"

"You thought I'd *what?*" her mother snapped before she could even finish her sentence. "You thought I'd be *happy* that my daughter is wasting time being followed around by a bunch of mindless Neanderthals with microphones rather than devoting her time to infinitely more important pursuits—like school, for instance. And what are you still doing up anyway? It must be after midnight there."

Yikes. She was definitely going to need backup on this one. Casey looked over at Nanna, who was sitting at the kitchen table, methodically making her way through a bag of Pepperidge Farm Mint Milanos while busily doing the crossword in a red felt-tipped pen. Obviously she was on her own.

"Oh, come on, Mom," Casey snapped, suddenly cranky from lack of sleep and the prospect of having to deal with her mother so late at night. "The only reason you even care is because it's TV. If I'd been chosen to lead some stuffy symposium on great books or something, you'd be wetting your pants in happiness." Casey knew that with the exception of PBS, Barbara McCloy considered television an inherent evil in contemporary society, capable of converting young minds to the capitalist agenda in just a few short hours. As a result, almost all of Casey's mass-media consumption had taken place at friends' houses after school, or in the wee hours after her mother went to bed at night.

"There is nothing academic about television," her mother said smugly. "It's for tiny people with tiny minds."

"Then I guess I'm one of them," Casey shot back, unable to keep her sarcasm in check. She didn't exactly know what it was about her mother that always seemed to rub her the wrong way. Maybe it was the fact that Barbara preferred to lecture rather than actually listen. Or maybe it was just that she was almost seventeen, and any even vaguely adult presence was bound to get on her nerves. Either way, she knew it was time to cut the conversation short. "Look, Mom," she began again, her voice calmer this time. "It's done. Nanna signed the papers, and I'm on the show, so you can either support me or not. It's your choice." Casey paused, listening to the silence filling the other end of the line.

"We'll discuss it over the holidays," Barbara said after a few moments, her tone still icy.

"You're coming . . . here?" Casey said in disbelief. Great. That was just what she needed to make her mess of a life even *more* complicated.

"Didn't Nanna tell you?" her mother asked, exasperation filling her voice. Casey could almost imagine her on the other end of the line, a cup of steaming Earl Grey at her elbow, her tortoiseshell glasses perched on the bridge of her nose, the morning paper strewn out before her on the kitchen table. "I'll be back on the twentieth."

"No," Casey said, shooting her grandmother a dirty look— not that she even noticed, so buried was she in her crossword and cookies. "She didn't mention it."

"Well, we'll discuss it then, so don't think for a moment that this subject is even remotely closed," Barbara added brusquely. There was a click as her mother hung up abruptly, then the humming sound of the empty line. Casey looked hard at the receiver in her hand then walked into the kitchen, placing it gently back into the cradle.

Casey couldn't believe her luck. Not only had everything gone completely sour with Drew, she'd gone and gotten butterflies from Darin, of all people, and her raging feminist-Marxist mother Barbara "I'm not a Communist dear, there's a difference" McCloy was coming to town for a visit. As she dragged her feet across the floor, past Nanna and her crumb-covered newspaper, on her way to bed, there was only one thing she could be certain of—it was all bound to make great television.

cold as ice

"So what's going on, Drew? It didn't look like you guys were exactly . . . studying," Robert Van Allen said with a half-grin, sitting down on the edge of Drew's rumpled, post-sex bed, one hand stroking his salt-and-pepper beard the way he always did when he was worried about something, or deep in thought. Drew pulled a navy sweatshirt roughly over his head and crossed his arms over his chest, glaring at his father before responding, his murky blue eyes dull with anger.

"Maybe we were and maybe we weren't," he said coolly, the frozen core of his fury melting rapidly in the small room, the force it still held surprising him. "But either way, it's not really any of your business." As soon as the words fell from his lips, Drew felt immediately disoriented. *Who is this person,* he thought to himself as he watched a look of surprise moving over his father's face like a heavy velvet curtain coming down between them, *talking to my father like this?*

"Drew," his father said gently, his eyes tired and red as if he'd been crying recently. When Drew had woken up early that morning, stumbling out to the kitchen for some orange juice, he'd found his father sitting in the living room, looking out at the dawn breaking over the Manhattan skyline, stroking his beard, clearly lost in thought. Looking at his father now, Drew wondered for the first time if he'd even been sleeping through the night since his mother had left for London. "You're my son," his dad said with a quiet finality. But strangely, in spite of his father's calmness, his obvious exhaustion, Drew felt the anger inside him building, threatening to boil over completely, spilling, unchecked, out of his mouth before he could do anything to stop it. It was the way he had always reacted in moments like these. The more reasonable anyone became when he was pissed off, the angrier Drew inevitably got. "And what you do under this roof is most definitely my business. And *this*"—Drew's father gestured at the rumpled bed—"just isn't *like you,* Drew."

"Maybe it's *exactly* like me," Drew blurted out, his hands coming down to rest at his sides and balling into fists as he continued. "I mean, isn't indiscreet sexual behavior kind of a Van Allen trademark?" he added nastily, the bitterness and sarcasm he'd been trying to bury inside him filling the room before he could put it in check. The part of Drew that was immediately sorry the minute the words left his mouth cringed as he watched his father's face turn red as the beefsteak tomatoes waiting patiently on the kitchen counter. But the part of him that was still furious positively gloated at the marked change in his father's expression.

"Drew, listen," his father barked, standing up and reaching toward him with one hand, his patience clearly at its limit. "I know you're still angry with me, but this has got to *stop*."

Oh really? Drew thought with a smile that rapidly morphed into a grimace, *is that what you told yourself when you were fucking Mrs. Reynaud?* There were some things that, no matter how angry he might be, Drew would never dare to say aloud in his father's presence. This was definitely one of them. Drew swallowed the unsaid sentence like a spoonful of bitter medicine, and shoved his hands into his pockets, looking down at the floor to avoid his father's penetrating gaze.

"Whatever you say, *Dad*," Drew answered, his voice wooden and devoid of feeling. Drew looked at the foot or so of parquet that separated him from his father, and wondered how a distance so short had suddenly grown so wide. Just a few weeks ago he and his dad would've talked calmly about this whole thing with Mad—maybe even laughed about it. Now they were almost at blows—or, at least Drew was, his hands curled into fists at his sides. "But I think you're the last person who should be judging anyone right now."

Drew grabbed his Timbuk2 messenger bag from the floor as he spoke, his voice shaking, and threw his black cashmere Marc Jacobs coat over one arm. He knew if he didn't get out of here soon, one of two things might happen. He'd either cry, or break something, and right now, either option sounded equally terrible. If he didn't leave now, he knew he might say something that he wouldn't be able to take back—and that his father might never forget. Before his dad could say anything else, Drew walked quickly out into the hall and through the front door, slamming it behind him.

As soon as the cold shock of outside air hit him, Drew felt his pulse begin to slow slightly, thrumming in his veins less and less insistently as he stood there on the sidewalk in front of his building, trying to just breathe. He looked up at the bright lights burning in his apartment, way up on top of the city he loved most in the world, and wondered how a place that had always felt so much like home could suddenly feel so otherworldly. Drew took a deep breath and tried to concentrate on the sensation of the icy air moving in and out of his lungs, trying not to think about what a mess his life was lately, and how he kept screwing everything up—first with Casey, and now with Mad—again. Now with his parents' marriage in the toilet, his life seemed to be on a continuous loop of 24/7 bad.

As he watched the light in his parents' bedroom go out, the window turning rapidly dark, he turned in the bracing air and walked toward the park, his footsteps quickening as he moved, his nose running onto his upper lip. If he could just walk fast enough, maybe he could get far enough away from this whole mess so that it wouldn't matter anymore. Maybe if his feet just kept moving, he'd be able to make some sense out of the thoughts that were crowding themselves together in his skull. He wiped his face with one hand and silently willed himself to get it together. *It's just the cold air*, he told himself as he felt his eyes burning with unshed tears. He blinked them back rapidly, his dark eyelashes hitting his cheeks as he walked into the entrance to the park, the shuffling of his footsteps on pavement and the wind howling down the block almost drowning out the sound of his heartbeat reverberating in his ears.

the breakfast club

Madison sat at the round, highly polished mahogany table in the Macallisters' buttercup-yellow breakfast room, a small, cut-crystal bowl of raspberries, blueberries, and low-fat vanilla yogurt in front of her. She dipped her spoon into the mixture repeatedly, covering the silver surface with gloopy yogurt, then letting it slide off the spoon back into the bowl, uneaten. She had absolutely no idea why Edie insisted on having a morning meal together one day a week, considering the fact that her mother could barely open her eyes before noon, much less participate in anything as banal as breakfast. Besides, the only things she'd ever seen Edie actually ingest on a regular basis were caviar, champagne, and Valium—not exactly the breakfast of champions.

Madison looked over at Edie, who was seated clear at the other end of the glossily polished table, wearing a billowing black velvet floor-length Bill Blass robe with enormous bat wing sleeves that were sure to dip into her own bowl of imported toasted rice cereal from Italy, and skim milk that was so fat-free it looked totally blue against the white Limoges china it currently floated in. Edie's blond hair fell to her shoulders, and without makeup her skin looked as white as an albino in a snowstorm. Edie reached for a prescription bottle in the center of the table, her sleeves dragging across the tabletop, and opened it, popping a few small yellow pills in her mouth and swallowing hard before looking up at her daughter and frowning. Well, as much as she could, considering her forehead had recently turned to stone with all the Botox injections she'd been getting in an attempt to ward off Father Time with poisonous chemicals. Madison knew that frown. It was the same look Edie had always given her when they were about to discuss something "serious," and chances were it would definitely be something Madison had absolutely no desire to talk about. At all.

"Darling," Edie began, her voice husky with sleep, and probably too much champagne the night before. "I've made a decision. As far as I'm concerned, leaving your future in your own hands is absolutely suicidal. Which is why I've signed you up for a college admission training session with that *wonderful* tutor Phoebe's mother has hired. You know"—Edie's voice dropped to a whisper—"I hear she helped get Maxine Vandenberg into *Princeton*."

Madison rolled her eyes and pushed her bowl away, crossing her arms over her deep purple Marc Jacobs velvet blazer. Maxine Vandenberg was so hopelessly clueless that it was amazing she didn't get flattened by a cement truck every time she crossed the fucking street. *Thanks for the vote of confidence, Mom,* Madison intoned silently. Okay, so she definitely wasn't Albert Einstein or anything, but she wasn't a drooling moron like Maxine Vandenberg either. There was a big difference.

"Perhaps studying with Phoebe will help keep you motivated," Edie added, raising a glass of freshly squeezed orange juice to her lips, then setting it back down on the table with a grimace. "And I'm certainly not leaving you getting into Harvard to chance." Edie shuddered, an expression of distaste drawing the corners of her mouth downward. "In any case," she added crisply, "your first joint session is this afternoon, and I think it goes without saying that you had better be there. Is that clear?"

"Crystal," Mad said grumpily, wondering exactly what Edie was going to do when she found out that instead of showing up at the Reynauds' apartment for her "training session" she'd spent the afternoon being beautified at Bliss with a seaweed wrap and a hot stone pedicure. *She'll probably have an aneurysm,* Mad thought with a slow, catlike smile.

"Because I have absolutely no qualms cutting you off financially if you fail to get into an acceptable college," Edie said mildly, bringing a spoonful of cereal to her mouth and chewing thoughtfully as she stared into the distance.

"And I suppose acceptable means *Harvard*, right?" Madison

snapped, feeling a wave of apprehension so deep it felt almost like nausea. Cut her off? Was she serious? When it came to Edie, one could never be sure. Edie spent most of her waking hours in such a deep chemical haze that she was utterly unpredictable. One day she'd be planning a trip to a Buddhist retreat in Oregon, and then the next week she'd be waxing ecstatically about some new mud bath in Tahiti she'd read about, Oregon and Buddhism apparently long forgotten.

"Of *course!*" Edie snapped back, rolling her hazel eyes that were so bloodshot they looked almost entirely red in color. "Really, Madison—is that even a question?"

Madison sighed loudly, watching as her mother began to stare dreamily into space, humming to herself, her "morning vitamins" obviously kicking in. Whenever Madison thought about the next year, the ridiculous frenzy of applying to colleges, she wanted to drink straight vodka until she threw up, then take a big nap that would stretch on until she was twenty-five—at least. What was the point of going to an Ivy League school in the first place when she had absolutely no idea what she wanted to do with her life? When she looked into the future, try as she might to see some kind of career for herself, she saw nothing but a looming, dark space—and that complete and total lack of information was one of the only things that scared Madison Macallister shitless.

How am I supposed to know if I want to go to Harvard, when I don't even know what I want to do with my life, she brooded silently, refusing to make eye contact with her mother, who blinked vaguely at her over the enormous centerpiece of white lilies and roses that dominated the center of the table, the overly sweet stench of the flowers making Madison's stomach turn crazily. *Maybe it's time you found out,* a little voice at the back of her brain whispered, as she stood up, teetering unsteadily on her heels, *before you wind up as whacked out as Edie.*

"Oh, and don't forget about the Holiday Gala at the Guggenheim next week," Edie called out just as Madison was about to walk out of the room.

Madison stopped dead in her tracks, placing her hands on her hips, which were covered in a matching purple Marc Jacobs tweed mini, and spun around, her black Cesare Paciotti ankle boots skidding on the parquet floor, her legs covered in black textured Dior stockings she'd borrowed from Edie's well-stocked lingerie drawer. "But that's the night *De-Luxe* premieres on Pulse!" she wailed, unable to comprehend the depth of Edie's horribleness.

The Holiday Gala at the Guggenheim was the most unbelievably boring event on earth. Like she really needed to stand around with a bunch of tight-ass Upper East Side debutantes *again* this year, and listen to them yak on endlessly about where they were applying for college, and how high their GPAs were this term. The thought of it made her want to drive a butter knife through her own skull, just to avoid the whole thing. She could almost picture herself convalescing in the hospital, her room filled with flowers, a white bandage wrapped around her perfectly coiffed brunette head as she stared blankly into space, a glazed expression in her lushly mascaraed eyes. Drew would be sitting at the side of the bed, his head in his hands, a worried expression creasing his gorgeous face. *Please, Madison,* she could almost hear him whispering as she lay there, totally unresponsive, staring up at the ceiling, *I'm sorry for being such an ass face, but now I know that I want to be with you forever. Won't you please, please come back to me?*

Edie smirked, raising the orange juice to her lips and finally taking a sip. "That's why God invented TiVo."

Madison stomped off, her chocolate brown hair flying around her face as she slammed the front door behind her, hoping to God that the Guggenheim had exceptionally dull butter knives. She planned on calling the hospital in advance, to make sure they had the TiVo set to record.

california
dreaming

⊖

Sophie St. John hurried up the steps of Meadowlark
Academy, tripping over the slick granite while silently cursing
the pristine and slippery soles of her new winter-white Tod's
ankle boots. But they were so infinitely cute that she couldn't
not wear them—especially when she had the most gorgeous
Marni faux-fur jacket in eggshell to match . . . Sophie exhaled loudly, blowing her honey-colored bangs from her face,
irritated to find that despite the fact that she'd showered less
than an hour before, she was already kind of damp and
sweaty from practically running the five short blocks to
school.

　She wasn't sure how it happened, but no matter what she
did, she was chronically late. It was a total mystery, considering

that every night she set her baby pink Hello Kitty alarm clock for seven A.M. without fail, and every morning she found herself rolling over and sleepily hitting the snooze button—then jumping out of bed a half hour later, her heart knocking in her chest. She would then inevitably wind up racing to the bathroom and jumping into the shower whispering a chorus of *shitshitshit* under her breath while she rubbed L'Occitane lavender shower gel over her body so fast it almost gave her the spins. The perfect gloriousness of her morning culminated with running around her room dripping wet and throwing clothes around like an escaped mental patient on a shopping spree at Barneys. "I should learn to meditate or something," Sophie mumbled under her breath and she reached the top of the steps, stopping to push her now dampened hair from her face. Just as she was about to push open the heavy blue doors, a horn beeped loudly behind her.

A black limousine idled at the curb, exhaust poofing discreetly from the rear exhaust pipe in quiet, gray plumes that drifted through the early morning air like fog. The driver's-side door opened, and a man in a sleek black uniform stepped out, a black cap covering his graying hair.

"Miss St. John?" he yelled out, cupping his hands, encased in black leather gloves, around his mouth. He motioned with one arm for Sophie to approach the car, and she tripped back down the stairs, her brow wrinkling with confusion. Was this maybe one of those drive-by kidnapping cases she'd heard about on the news lately? Although she couldn't imagine that kidnappers would rent a black limo for the sole purpose of snatching a young girl off the streets of the Upper East Side, would they? As Sophie approached the car, the black, tinted window on the passenger's side rolled quietly down, revealing the sleek, blond head of Sophie's biological mother, Melissa Von Norton, her hair streaming like a waterfall to shoulders that were wrapped in a crimson Pashmina, her sharply chiseled face half-hidden by an enormous pair of Roger Vivier python sunglasses with shiny gold buckles adorning each earpiece. But behind the dark lenses, Sophie knew, were bottle-glass green eyes, the exact same hue and shape as her own.

"Sophie," Melissa said, her slightly raspy voice like chocolate dipped in caramel. "Would you get in for a moment? I'd really like to speak to you."

Sophie crossed her arms over the immaculate wool of her Marni jacket, tucking her hands firmly under her arms. "I'm late for school," she answered, trying to make her voice sound as neutral as possible. But despite her best efforts, when the sentence left her lips it still came out clipped, awkward, and slightly angry.

Melissa removed her dark shades, and her eyes glowed out of the darkness of the limo like twin green spotlights. "I'll write you a note," she said smoothly, swinging open the car door. "Isn't that what mothers do?" she added with a half-smile.

"How would *you* know?" Sophie shot back as she shifted her weight from one booted foot to the other. She could already tell that by the end of the day, no matter how cute they were, her Tod's boots were going to be the bane of her existence—her feet would probably be covered in blisters that would force her to hobble around the halls like an uncoordinated moron.

Melissa sighed heavily, looking down at her perfectly glossed fingernails that were painted the palest shade of pink. "I *don't* know, Sophie," she said finally, looking up and locking eyes with her daughter. "But I am *trying* to learn—if you'll give me a chance."

Sophie stood there, the irritated expression she'd been wearing moments before rapidly sliding from her face. A million different emotions swept through her at once—fear, anger, and doubt in the lead, but confusion ultimately winning out, rapidly replacing all three in an instant. It was so totally typical of the mess that was currently her life—just when she thought she'd made up her mind to hate her biological mother, Melissa showed up and said something that made the entire enterprise seem utterly impossible.

"I have five minutes," Sophie said grudgingly, giving in and climbing into the backseat, determined to hold on to the memory of her anger no matter *what* Melissa had to say.

"Okay," Melissa said, a relieved expression sweeping over her face as Sophie sat back on the plush leather seat, crossing her arms over her chest again, ready for battle.

"So, what do you want?" Sophie asked in a tone that made her mother immediately tense up again. Sophie watched as Melissa crossed her long legs encased in dark denim that fit snugly to her lithe body.

"I want to talk about what happened at your party." Melissa took a deep breath, leaning forward slightly in her seat, the collection of gold bangles on her wrist jangling like her own personal movie soundtrack. The closer she got, the more Sophie found it difficult to look away from her mother's face. It wasn't just that Melissa Von Norton had a face that had lit up millions of silver screens around the world, it was that looking at Melissa was like looking into some kind of strange funhouse mirror where all the best parts of herself were reflected back at her—the finely sloped nose, the high cheekbones and long, tapered fingers. Looking at her mother was like looking at some computer-generated representation of her ideal self. It made Sophie feel weirdly connected to Melissa, but also a bit dejected. Melissa Von Norton represented a kind of perfection that Sophie, with her mottled collection of paper-thin, white-and-freshly-red scars marring the smooth surface of her arms, could never hope to attain. Sophie looked down, her stomach jumping in her lap, and was relieved to see that the ivory cuffs of her coat completely covered her marred wrists.

"I never meant to use you for publicity, Sophie." Melissa stopped and cleared her throat, then swallowed hard before continuing. "Things just got out of control."

"That's an understatement, don't you think?" Sophie snapped, turning to gaze out the window at a homeless man who was bent all the way over, digging at the bottom of a metal trash can. Her sweet sixteen party should've been the best night of her life—a night she should've remembered forever. She'd remember it all right—but because it had been a complete disaster. She'd ended up running out into the street, dodging passing cars, tears burring her vision, just to get away from the hordes of reporters, the flashes of light, and a mother who was more than happy to use her as a photo op, who thought she could buy the affection of a daughter she'd never laid eyes on with something as tacky as a new car.

"Okay, look," Melissa said exasperatedly, pushing the curtain of blond hair from her face, raking the silky strands back with splayed fingers. "I did invite *some* press to the event, but I thought I could control things. I thought we'd have *plenty* of time to ourselves. But I guess I was wrong." Melissa sat back with a sigh, her expression suddenly weary.

"Do you have any idea how excited I was to meet you?" Sophie said quietly, her eyes still locked on the window. "How much I looked forward to it? For weeks it was all I could think about."

"Weeks?" Melissa gave a short laugh and bit her bottom lip. Her beautiful, angular face contorted in pain. "I've thought about you every day since the moment you left my arms," she said quietly. "Every day."

"Really?" Sophie said in a voice so small it was barely audible—even in the close confines of the backseat. She turned to face her mother, her anger and sadness melting away when she saw the pain in Melissa's eyes, the emotion clouding the clear green of her gaze.

"Yes, really," Melissa said, the corners of her lips curling up in her trademark smile, her full pink lips parting.

"The why did you wait so long to find me?" Sophie wondered aloud, leaning forward slightly.

"Your mother and I had an agreement," Melissa said simply, shrugging her slim, cashmere-swaddled shoulders. "And the last thing I wanted to do was complicate your life."

"But you're here now," Sophie said slowly, watching as Melissa reached into her black Hermès Birkin bag on the seat next to her for a tissue, the glossy leather gleaming in the morning light. Melissa dabbed at the corners of her eyes, carefully navigating the subtle streaks of aubergine liner that made her green eyes pop.

"I am," she agreed. "And I'm sorry that we got off on the wrong foot. I want to try to make things up to you." Melissa threw the tissue back in her bag and leaned forward, taking Sophie's hands in her own. "*If* you'll let me."

At the touch of her mother's hands, Sophie felt as helpless as a kitten to refuse, or stay angry. Like it or not, this woman was a part of her—a part she didn't know anything about. Sophie didn't know if they were going to ever have any kind of traditional mother/daughter relationship—whatever that was—but she did know that she wanted to try. After all, what did she have to lose? *Your heart, maybe*, she thought as Melissa's fingers tightened around her own. *After all, if she broke it once . . .*

Sophie tried to push the thought out of her mind as she shook her head briskly, her honey blond hair swinging around her face. "So, how are you going to do that? Make it up to me, I mean," she said with a wry smile.

"Well," her mother began excitedly, dropping Sophie's hands and waving her own long finger expansively in the air,

"I thought you might come out for Christmas this year—that way we could spend some real time getting to know one another, just you and me."

"Come out . . ." Sophie began slowly, "to *California*?"

"That's where I live, you know," Melissa said wryly, one side of her mouth tilted into a small smile. "I'm starting work on a film in early January, but I thought you could hang out with me on set in between takes. In any case, we'll have a lot of time before the shoot begins to get to know one another."

"But . . . I always spend the holidays with my family," Sophie said quickly, the words leaving her lips before she could think about how they might sound. There was a pause as Melissa looked down at her denim-clad knees and began to pick at a stray thread.

"Right," she said woodenly, her voice expressionless. "Your family. Of course."

"I'm sorry," Sophie said, reaching across and placing her hand on top of her mother's cold fingers. "I'm not used to all of this," she said helplessly. "I feel like I'm always saying all the wrong things."

Melissa looked up, relief washing over her features. "Me, too," she admitted, the small lines around her eyes crinkling with her change of expression. "What do you say we start over?"

"Okay," Sophie said, smiling. "How do we do that?"

"Think about coming to visit me over Christmas," Melissa answered, sitting back and sliding her sunglasses over her eyes again. "Why don't you have your parents call me and we'll discuss it. After all," she added with a grin, "they've had you for sixteen Christmases already—maybe they wouldn't mind giving up just one."

Sophie stared at her mother, visions of palm trees, winter sunshine, and movie sets dancing in her brain like sugar-coated celluloid flickering across the darkened screen of her mind. If she thought hard enough, she could smell the Bain de Soleil, the warm salt air drifting across the crystal-blue water . . .

"By the way." Melissa's voice cut into her thoughts, suddenly breaking her reverie. "Pulse called last week," Melissa said carefully. "They asked me to be on an episode of *De-Luxe* with you."

Sophie's eyes narrowed, her arms crossing over her chest again in a defensive reflex. *I knew it was too good to be true,* she told herself dejectedly, the excitement draining from her body in a rush of sadness. *She's an actress—of course she fooled me. That's her job, isn't it?*

"But, of course I said no," Melissa said, her voice as calm and flippant as if they were discussing something as innocuous as the weather. "I told them that my relationship with my daughter was private, and that I wouldn't dream of exploiting it."

"You did?" Sophie said aloud, her expression dazed. She felt like she'd just woken up from a bad dream that had dragged on for weeks on end. Melissa removed the shades again, and stared hard at her daughter, her gaze suddenly fierce.

"Sophie, you're *not* a photo op or publicity stunt for me—you're my daughter and I think it's about time we got to know one another, don't you?"

Sophie nodded, the beginnings of a smile spreading over her face, which she knew must look as flushed and happy as she felt. Tingles ran up and down her arms as she closed her eyes, picturing the bright California sunlight warming her cold, winterized skin, palm fronds waving in the breeze. She could almost see herself walking arm in arm with Melissa down Rodeo Drive, driving to Venice Beach, the top down on the black convertible BMW Melissa would surely have, the surf crashing at the shore, the golden sand sparkling in the tangy, salt-scented air. Of course there would be parties and premieres at night, and more stars in front of her face than in the smog-drenched sky. As she closed her eyes to see it all the more perfectly, Sophie couldn't help but let her once-tentative smile widen into a full-out grin.

uncomfortable
silences

⊖

"Winter break in Bel Air!" Sophie waved her hands in the air excitedly, deep violet nail polish winking in the light, her normally cream-colored complexion tinged with rose. "Melissa says she wants to have an old-fashioned family Christmas—whatever *that* means."

"I'm sure there'll be enough plastic trees *and* tits to go around." Madison took a careful sip of the steaming skinny mocha she was balancing on one palm—hold the whipped cream, thank you very much—and tried not to imagine stabbing Sophie in the eye with a spork, or some other semi-sharp object. She looked around at the stainless steel kiosks, the comforting, slightly sterile sameness of the Dining Hall, her green eyes searching out anything to pull her away from

Sophie's endless rambling about lunches at Spago, getting a tattoo from Kat Von D and other random Californicated, fake-baked madness.

But as she paid less and less attention, the thing Madison wanted to avoid most of all kept popping up—last night. After all, how many times *could* she lose her virginity to just one guy? Madison wasn't sure she wanted to keep pondering, much less actually attempting to answer that very sticky question. It was terrifying on way too many levels. If you had asked her the year before, she would've shot you a withering glare, dismissing such stupid questions with a heat-seeking missile of an insult—something about the person being a virgin and poorly dressed and a total fucking idiot—but cool and calculated, totally effortless, and thus completely effective. Still, your first time was your first time was your first time and, for a girl like Madison, it could never, ever be anything short of perfection. Yet here she was having had a first-first and a second-first and *both* had been unmitigated disasters. Was she sexually doomed? Would she spend the rest of high school losing her virginity to Drew over and over again in one terrible, embarrassing night after another? *Proper usage of the word unmitigated*, Mad thought, smiling slightly despite suddenly feeling like she was going to cry right there in the stupid Dining Hall, in front of the entire world. At least the half-hearted prepping she'd done in anticipation of the SATs was *definitely* starting to pay off.

"It'll be just like an episode of *The Hills*," Phoebe said dreamily. "You'll probably spend break sitting on verandas drinking twelve-dollar bottles of mineral water, and eating goat cheese and sun-dried tomato pizzas with Brody Jenner all day long." Phoebe pushed up the sleeves of her Tracey Ross sage green mohair sweater, her nearly jet-black hair swinging to her shoulders like an outtake from a shampoo commercial.

"Well, if that's the case, I guess your nail polish will start magically changing from pink to black—in all of ten minutes," Madison snapped, referring to the show's obvious continuity errors.

Casey laughed, draining the last of her bottle of Evian and capping it with a twist of her wrist. Madison couldn't help but notice that, first off, Evian just *happened* to be the word *naïve* spelled backward, and, secondly, that Casey looked happy— not to mention almost fashionable in a white Calvin Klein sweater dress and a pair of Etienne Aigner black riding boots— courtesy of Pulse, of course. It wasn't like Casey, financial neophyte that she was, could actually afford the thousands of dollars' worth of clothes currently swathing her traitorous, almost-boyfriend-stealing body. That being said, every time Madison looked at the formerly psychotically curly-haired ex-Midwesternite lately, her growing wardrobe was a bit of a shock. Putting Casey in designer clothes was kind of like sticking a pony in a tutu—totally bizarre. Madison didn't know what annoyed her more: the fact that Casey was rapidly approaching pretty, the weirdness of seeing her all done up in designer labels notwithstanding, or her obvious happiness. Every option made her want to run screaming from the room. Was it Darin who was putting that high-pro glow into those corn-fed cheeks of hers? *I guess stranger things have definitely happened*, Madison mused, as she watched Casey pull a large chocolate-chocolate-chunk cookie from a white paper bag.

"My mom did a talk at USC once, something about gender roles in medieval texts. One of her typically feminist rants. Anyway, I was supposed to go with her, but I had to play in a violin recital the same day, so I never went. You're so lucky, Sophs—you'll be able to go to the Getty and everything."

Madison watched as Casey broke apart the cookie with her fingers, and popped a piece in her mouth, closing her eyes and chewing rapturously. Madison pushed her salmon salad around on her plate resentfully, the way she did during every lunch hour. She couldn't even so much as *look* at a cookie without gaining ten pounds, and sometimes it really annoyed her. She wondered for the millionth time what it would be like to throw caution to the wind and just eat every fucking thing she wanted—regardless of calorie count and fat gram content. *Sometimes being a teen icon is totally exhausting*, she thought, bringing her mocha up to her lips and sipping slowly, pretending it was a cheeseburger.

"What's the Getty?" Phoebe said, scrunching up her forehead and looking at Casey like she'd just suggested eating bugs for breakfast. "Is that the nouvelle fusion place on Robertson with the totally weird lighting? They have the *best* Niçoise salad there!"

"Seriously?" Sophie asked excitedly, pulling her honey blond hair back and securing it with a tortoiseshell barrette so that her heart-shaped face was fully exposed, her naturally pale skin gleaming softly. "I think I read about that place in *W*. I'm definitely going!"

Casey laughed, her cheeks flushing a deep rose, her straight yellow hair shining under the scarily fluorescent lights of the Dining Hall.

God, they had fucking Thomas Keller designing their lunch menu—was it impossible to get some decent fucking lighting, Madison thought as Casey composed herself, turning to face Sophie and Phoebe.

"It's a *museum*, you guys," she explained, rolling her eyes in Phoebe's direction. "Not a restaurant."

"Oh," Sophie said with a dismissive wave of one thin, pale hand. "Why would I want to go *there*?"

"Oh, I don't know . . ." Casey began, a smile beginning to twitch at the corners of her lightly glossed lips. "For some culture, maybe?"

"Culture?" Sophie shot back with a giggle, waving one pale hand dismissively. "I get enough of that right here in Manhattan."

"Really," Phoebe added as she removed a Chantecaille compact from her Cesare Paciotti caramel leather hobo bag and cracked it open to survey her predictably perfect visage in the tiny mirror.

Madison didn't know what was more annoying—the fact that her recent devirginization was such a disaster . . . again—or listening to Casey, Sophie, and Phoebe yak about meaningless bullshit every chance they got when she had *real* problems . . . But before she could truly ponder the seriousness of that question, Drew entered the Dining Hall, looking the way he always did lately—depressed. *Make that barely conscious,* Madison thought as she watched Drew meander his way through the crowded room, barely cracking a smile until he reached the Whole Bean kiosk, where he proceeded to stand in line, staring longingly at the selection of fragrant, slightly oily coffee beans in a series of large plastic containers behind the counter like they contained the answer to his life's woes.

Drew did not look like a guy who'd had the astonishingly good fortune to have gotten laid just twelve short hours ago. In fact, he looked like a guy who had spent his formative years locked away in a Turkish prison, and about as far away from the inarguably blissful sight of Madison Macallister strategically draped in shreds of satin and lace as he could get. But the completely irritating thing about Drew was that no matter how strenuously he moped along the halls of Meadowlark, no matter how greasy his hair got or how many times he wore the same stupid green Ralph Lauren sweater with the rip in the elbow, he still looked uncomfortably, unbearably hot. Drew paused in front of their table, his eyes meeting hers and then dropping to the floor. He took a sip of his coffee and moved forward, a grim expression clouding his face.

"Hey, guys," Drew said, his speech a flat monotone. Madison stared back at him with a look she felt to be a close approximation of his voice, but without all that whiny emo bullshit. A look that would turn a fresh, blooming red rose jet-black, but without irony, poetry, or some symptom of the dark and twisted world that tortured his dark and twisted soul. No matter how much Drew's presence habitually set her unmentionables on fire, Madison was so *done* with his dark and stormy bullshit. From now on, she'd only go for skulls and crossbones if they happened to be set in platinum and studded in diamonds.

"Mad, Casey," Drew said, nodding to each corner of his love triangle as Sophie and Phoebe continued to talk about California, discussing the finer points of L.A.-based reality television and wondering why they called it *The Hills* when Los Angeles was so obviously on the beach, completely oblivious to his presence. Mad just kept on with her whole *I am killing plants with my gaze, and I don't give a shit* thing while Casey attempted to look nonplussed, one eye pretending to drift aimlessly around the room while they other quivered around, looking at Drew and looking away again and again and again.

"I see that, uh, we're drinking coffee," Drew went on after a moment of silence between the three, his voice pushed and labored, trying too hard to sound safe, funny, and likeable. "I hear that's, like, totally the new thing to do. This whole coffee thing—the black stuff, the brown stuff, or the white stuff." Drew sat down next to Casey at the far end of the table, and drummed his fingers on the table while staring at his cup.

Both of the girls continued to sit in silence, Mad stock-still except for the tip of one perfectly manicured finger that she was running around the rim of her cup. Casey, on the other hand, was shaking and shivering like a baby rabbit, one foot tap, tap, tapping manically against the base of her chair, a small quiver at the corner of her mouth showing how badly she wanted to talk to Drew, and how much it was killing her to hold back.

"You know what, I feel exactly the same way," Drew said, holding up his end of the nonexistent conversation. "It's like, how could you drink that many Frappuccinos in one day? I think it's all a conspiracy theory. That it's not really her in all the pictures, but a small group of well-disguised aliens *dressed up* as Britney Spears. Remember the whole bald thing? Totally an alien."

Mad imagined that if her life had suddenly been transformed into a bad teen comedy—which, come to think of it, would definitely explain *a lot* about the whole virginity doover disaster—the sound track would've had crickets chirping in the background right about then. She had moved from tracing the cup's rim to swirling around her last few sips of mocha, and the rolling, milky coffee that pulled back to show a few sparse grounds on the cup's bottom had Mad wondering if it was at all possible for those grains to tell her anything about her future or what she should do about Drew.

"Yeah, that Britney . . . she's probably dead at this point. But don't think we'll stop seeing her and all of the frappés and craziness anytime soon. They'll just send down more and more of the aliens and put 'em in Britney suits. Maybe they'll eventually figure out the finer points of their construction and we'll have Hot Britney back again for good. But who knows. Anyway, it's been great talking to you guys, but I've got to head to class."

Drew got up, throwing his blue-and-yellow Timbuk2 messenger bag over one shoulder, and then stood there awkwardly before opening his mouth again and looking expectantly in Madison's direction. *It's about fucking time*, Madison fumed to herself, raising her left eyebrow and trying to throw her best how-are-you-going-to-make-this-up-to-me vibe in his direction. Surely now he would take her by the hand and lead her to an intimate corner of the Dining Hall where he'd inform her that not only was last night the best night of his life, but that he loved her and only her. He'd then drop to one knee and profess his undying love, quoting Shakespearean sonnets and Elizabethan rhyming couplets until she died of embarrassment—or he'd just make out with her until her MAC Lipglass was hopelessly smudged. Either one would just about do.

But instead Drew dropped his gaze to the floor before turning to Casey, looking her dead in her gray eyes, and saying quietly, in a voice that was almost a mumble, "So, can I call you later, maybe?"

Madison felt like the room had just frozen over completely. Her mouth opened and closed, her light pink, heavily glossed lips sticking together, and then releasing. She shook her head briefly from side to side on the pretense of shaking out her hair to give it more volume. Was she going deaf? She couldn't be sure, but she *thought* she'd just heard Drew ask Casey if he could call her later. Because although Drew definitely owed Casey some kind of apology for acting like a horse's ass for the last month or so—as much as Madison hated to actually admit

119

it—his obligation to the girl he recently deflowered was much more pressing.

Casey's foot tapped faster, her mouth moving from quivering to a quake as she fought back the urge to blurt out an answer. Instead she fixed her gaze somewhere over Drew's head, her gray eyes distant and unfocused before she stared down at her almost empty latte cup, grabbing onto it like a life preserver and raising the lukewarm coffee to her lips. Drew, being predictably terrible at reading women—a skill he'd managed to actually get worse at over the years rather than better—obviously thought he was getting the cold shoulder. He quickly scooped up his still-steaming coffee from the table, and took off through the hall, not looking back.

Madison sat there in shock, still steaming a bit herself, trying to regain what was left of her composure. How. Dare. He. Well, that settled it—no matter what he said or did, no matter how much he begged, there was no way Drew was ever getting into the tangled, silken web of her La Perla again. *Count on it*, Madison thought, her green eyes suddenly watery. She grabbed a napkin from off the table and patted her nose delicately, trying not to draw too much attention to herself.

"Fucking allergies," she sniffed when Sophie and Phoebe turned to look in her direction, balling up the tissue in her fist and chucking it across the table littered with half-empty cups and plates. Mad rummaged around in her Coach hobo, trying to pretend like she was looking for something important, just so she could keep her head down to hide the tears that were rapidly welling up in her eyes. It was moments like these that made Madison wish more than anything that she had someone, anyone, she could trust enough to confide in. But even if she did, the thought of having to explain to anyone that she'd slept with Drew the night before, only to have him ignore her the next day and subsequently kiss Casey's ass during lunch, was too potentially humiliating to even contemplate.

"I think I'm allergic to milk," Sophie piped up, pushing away her empty vanilla latte, clearing her throat with an exaggerated cough. "Or maybe the air around here. *Something* is making me feel all phlegmy these days." Sophie grabbed her throat with one hand, massaging her smooth, pale skin with her fingers. "Whatever. I am *not* getting sick this close to Christmas."

"Maybe it's the noxious scent of your Designer Imposter's perfume," Madison snapped, crossing her arms over her chest.

"Bite your tongue," Sophie said with faux indignation, shuddering slightly. "You know perfectly well I only wear Missoni."

"I didn't know they sold Missoni at CVS now," Phoebe said contemplatively, a wicked glint in her dark eyes. "Huh."

Sophie rolled her eyes and began to giggle. "You guys suck," she said good-naturedly, smoothing her long bangs back from her face with a practiced hand. "So, what did the Drewster have to say for himself anyway?" Sophie and Phoebe started distractedly gathering up their books and brushing stray crumbs from their clothes, readying themselves for the end of lunch hour.

"Nothing interesting," Madison said darkly, stuffing her

leather notebook into her Coach bag. It was amazing—Madison always essentially viewed Meadowlark as the one place she was completely in control, and now, school had become just as—if not more—complicated as home. She'd given Drew everything a guy could ever want, and after all that he still preferred Casey. Madison Macallister could put up with a lot, but the sting of that kind of humiliation was not only inexplicable, but entirely too much to bear. If she couldn't live happily ever after with Drew, there was no way some Midwestern moron stuffed into designer clothes she didn't deserve was going to. No way. Once she told Casey what had happened between her and Drew last night, she doubted Casey would want to have anything to do with him ever again—much less pick up the phone and take his calls.

"So, Casey," Mad began, turning to face her and smiling sweetly. "What are you doing later tonight?"

Casey's mouth fell open slightly as she stared at Madison uncomprehendingly. Sophie's hand froze in midair as she was handing Phoebe a hot pink YSL lip gloss, the gold cap flashing in the light.

"*Me?*" Casey said after a long pause, pointing to her chest with one unpolished index finger. "Umm, not much. Studying, probably. The usual."

Madison stood up, shielding her eyes from the fluorescent glare with a pair of gold Dior aviators, the lenses tinted a rich, glowing amber. "Why don't you come over later?" she said airily, as if she issued such invitations on a regular basis. Madison threw her bag over one shoulder and looked over the top of her shades, her green eyes burning over the golden frames, one newly darkened brow arched imperiously. "We *definitely* need to talk."

the first cut is
the deepest . . .

"I mean, not shopping at Barneys isn't exactly going to put an end to the war in Iraq. I donated money to Obama's campaign this year and *everything*." Meadowlark junior Briana Sharp flipped her golden locks away from her perfectly tanned, oval face and smiled warmly into the camera, her bronze lip gloss sparkling. "So, I guess you could say I've done my part."

Drew couldn't help cracking a smile as he watched Briana's earnest face flickering at the front of the classroom gradually fade to black, and his own name outlined in bright white illuminating the now-darkened screen. Drew felt the hair on his arms stand up in a rush of pride mixed with excitement, and his stomach felt like it had suddenly been infiltrated by a band of alien invaders who were hell-bent on performing somersaults and back flips after drinking a bottle of Mad Dog. Drew rubbed his blue eyes, which were now tinged with red, a spider's web of broken blood vessels that made his eyes feel like they were full of sand. He'd barely slept at all last night. Instead of allowing himself to drift off into oblivion, he'd laid in bed until well after three A.M., the soothing sounds of Goldfrapp's *Seventh Tree* streaming through his earbuds doing nothing to slow his adrenaline as he lay there obsessively mulling over what Paxil might say once the final credits rolled and the lights came up.

As much as he hated himself for it, Drew couldn't help but hold out some hope that the black-clad auteur might be so moved as to leave his famously caustic wit at the door for once, stunned into humble silence by the sheer virtuosity of Drew's cinematic skills. When he closed his eyes, Drew could almost see himself on the red carpet at the Venice Film Festival, brightly colored boats sailing by in the distance, the choppy blue water lapping at the shore, the spiky, gold-encrusted top of St. Mark's Basilica rising from the square like a mirage. Paxil would undoubtedly be busily eviscerating some unsuspecting reporter, and Drew would be staring down at his Pumas, too overwhelmed to even think about forming words as Jim Jarmusch, Robert Rodriguez, and maybe even Woody Allen—his favorite filmmaker of all time—made their way down the red carpet, so close that Drew could almost reach out and touch the sleeves of Allen's nubbly tweed jacket for luck . . .

A polite burst of applause scattered through the class as

Paul Paxil jumped from his seat on the side of the room and flicked on the overhead light with a flourish of his wrist, flooding the room in fluorescence. Drew blinked rapidly and looked down at the desk, his cheeks flushing bright red. Drew wasn't exactly socially retarded by any stretch of the imagination, but the one thing that made him uncomfortable beyond belief was praise. Not that he didn't want it, need it, and seek it out at all costs, despite being filled with self-loathing for doing so—he just never knew exactly how to *respond* to such effusiveness when it came his way, especially when it was about his own work.

"Well, Drew," Paxil said, his voice sounding level and calm, a perfectly cool register that seemed so right for words of praise spoken from up high. "You really did a fantastic job of eviscerating your peers. The contempt and disdain you have for them echoes throughout the entirety of this piece." *True,* Drew thought to himself, *so what he's basically saying is that my thesis is clear and that I'm getting my point across. Awesome.*

Paxil paused, perching one black denim–clad hip on the edge of the gleaming, rectangular stainless steel desk at the front of the room. Drew felt his heart race even faster in that small pause, feeling unable to wait any longer before hearing all of the wonderfulness that he had to say. "And while we don't *see* you in the film, those that you interview act as stand-ins, showing that even in your compiling of their thoughts and opinions, you're constructing yourself as an amalgam of them all—the ultimate monster."

Drew couldn't believe his ears. Was this really happening?

A monster? He shook his head in disbelief, too stunned to speak. He felt his mouth opening and closing without sound, suddenly dry as paper. It was supposed to be an exposé, a look inside the cloistered, revered world of money and power, showing its corrupt core with himself acting as the guide. "Uh, I . . ." Drew stuttered, feeling that if only he could find the right words he could make Paxil understand how much he had misunderstood—help him to see the true *genius* of the whole thing.

"Oh, did you have something to add, Drew?" Paxil said in mock surprise, still affecting that same cool tone, the tone that Drew was quickly realizing meant the exact *opposite* of what he had hoped for when the lights flooded the room.

"Uh, well, uh. That wasn't really the point." Drew felt himself beginning to sweat, the underarms of the black T-shirt he wore beneath an olive Triple Five Soul sweater quickly turning very damp indeed. "This isn't supposed to be about *me*—it's supposed to be about all of *this*," Drew said, waving his arms around the air for emphasis.

"All of *what*?" Paxil threw back, his eyes narrowing behind the heavy black glasses he habitually wore. "This world of wealth, power, and privilege that you are so very much a part *of*?"

"Well, yeah," Drew stammered again, feeling his face turn horribly, embarrassingly crimson as he felt the bodies in the classroom around him tense up in anticipation, his peers suddenly at full attention. "I mean, that's what I was trying to *expose*."

"I see," Paxil said thoughtfully, sitting on top of the desk and crossing one leg over the other, his dirty black Converse swinging in the air. "And how did you think you were going to do so without acknowledging your *own* part in this world of excess and irresponsibility? How could you even hope to get your point across without explaining to the audience exactly where you see *yourself* fitting in?"

Drew sat there, nervously pulling at a loose thread of his APC jeans, and wondered if Paxil, as much as Drew despised him at this very moment for singling him out and embarrassing him, didn't actually have a point. Wasn't the whole idea of making the film to attempt to understand his admittedly complicated feelings about his own family's wealth and status? Instead of really exploring exactly where Drew Van Allen himself fit into the UES scene, the film had ended up a jumbled and judgmental collage of everyone else's opinions but his own. Paxil was right—there was no way he could keep himself at arm's length from his subjects, not when he was actually one of them! Drew bit his lip, grateful for the sharp pain that served as a momentary distraction from the fact that he was suddenly scarily close to losing it in front of everyone. His eyes burned in their sockets, and he blinked a few times to try to clear them. The film was only proof of what he already knew—he'd lost sight of himself lately, and in more ways than one.

Paxil's face softened momentarily beneath the dark coating of three-day stubble. He removed his glasses and began polishing them absentmindedly on the bottom of his ragged black sweater. "I'm not saying this to upset you, Drew," Paxil said matter-of-factly. "What I'm trying to do is to get you to see the larger *picture* here. There's no way you can make a successful documentary if you don't examine all sides of the issue and figure out where you stand *before* you get behind the camera. As a filmmaker, you have a responsibility not just to your audience, but to *yourself.*" Paxil's eyes held Drew's own for an uncomfortably long time, until he cleared his throat with a sound so torturous and raspy that Drew wouldn't have been surprised to learn that the director had sprinkled ground glass on his Cheerios that morning. "Now," he said with a wry smile, clapping his hands together loudly to signal that Drew was finally out of the hot seat, "where's my next victim?"

Andrea Spain, the mousiest girl in the entire junior class, raised her hand meekly, as if she were afraid that Paxil might lop it off with the brute force of his honesty. From her hunched posture, and the blond hair that fell across her face, her insecurity about the DVD she held in one shaking hand was completely transparent. She might as well have been wearing a goddamn sign that read, YOU'RE PROBABLY GOING TO HATE THIS AS MUCH AS I DO. Paxil snatched the DVD from Andrea's limp fingers with predatory glee and turned it over in his hands with a smirk, clearly taking pleasure in Andrea's awkwardness before barking, "Lights!" at the back of the room.

Drew sighed as the lights flicked off again and the room was plunged once more into comforting darkness. The screen glowed white, filled with the tan, plasticky figure of a headless Barbie in all her nude, pneumatic perfection. Drew could hear

Paxil groan audibly as the first acoustic notes of Hole's "Doll Parts" began to blare from the speakers overhead. Sure, Drew was glad to be off the hook, but as a succession of dismembered Mattel toys rolled across the screen, he couldn't help but wonder if, in the quest for some kind of self-discovery, he'd managed to make more of a disaster of his life than ever. He knew, as much as he really despised the idea that he was going to have to come to terms with this whole mess his parents had made, that he'd somehow have to try to dig his way out of the mountain of resentment and anger he was currently trapped beneath. The problem was that he didn't really have anyone to really talk to about the way things were falling apart. Well, he had tried to talk to Madison, but they'd just ended up naked, and the last thing Drew really needed right now was more drama with Miss Expectations herself. Still, he knew that, much like with everything that happened between him and Mad, as usual, he definitely could've handled the whole thing better—*a lot* better.

From the way she'd acted at lunch today, it was clear that Madison really hated him this time—and with good reason. God, why did he have to act like such an asshole the minute he got within fifty feet of her? Was he acting out for the camera? Trying to get revenge on his family for putting him in this fucked-up position? He still didn't even know how he felt about the actual sex. The minute it was over panic had streamed through his body replacing the euphoria and adrenaline he'd been feeling only seconds earlier. All of a sudden he felt trapped—like he wanted to run out into traffic just to get away from, well, not exactly her, but just . . . everything. And by the way Casey had glared at him at lunch, it was painfully obvious that he'd really blown things with her, too. All he wanted to do was to call her and try to explain everything— but when he saw the mix of coldness and confusion staring out at him from the depths of Casey's gray eyes, something inside his chest began to throb uncomfortably, and he had to look away.

All emotions and preconceived notions aside, it was just the damned *size* of the thing that he couldn't handle. Not that the affair itself was big—it was a pretty small, simple thing, when it came down to it—the questions it raised shot out of Drew's mind at the rate that Paxil hurled criticisms. When? Where? How did it start? And how long had it been going on? were the first questions to pop up whenever he put his mind to the topic, which was all the time lately. And then there were the tentacles that shot out from the affair itself, the possible effects and impacts that it might have on the people Drew was closest to—as well as any number of people beyond that immediate circle. Drew scribbled at the edge of his desk with a pen, taking perverse pleasure in the black ink that was rapidly staining the light wooden surface.

And what about Phoebe? Did Phoebe *know*, Drew wondered as his pen scratched across the desk. Or was she just as clueless as he had been, thinking that her parents were, well, her parents—instead of the pair of strangers that Drew had discovered his own to be. Strangers with ideas and ethics and emotions and fuck buddies that were apparently more important than that wonderful thing they used to have, the thing that most people call family—the thing that Drew now referred to as a sorry lie.

As messy images of doll mutilation scrolled across the screen, Drew released the pen and picked up his iPhone, surreptitiously pulling up MySpace and clicking on Phoebe's page. Phoebe grinned out at him from her profile pic, which featured a softly smiling Pheebs looking out from a pair of silver D&G shades that were so enormous, they made her head look about the size of a peanut. Before he could think too much about it, Drew clicked on the "messaging" icon and began hitting the keys with practiced fingers, worried that if he slowed down for even a moment to think about what exactly he was really doing, that he'd end up just bagging the whole thing altogether.

Hey Pheebs,
I know this is kind of random, but can we meet up later and talk?
Peace Out,
—DVA

candy stripping

"Well, the situation's not entirely hopeless—yet." Andrea Cavalli flipped through Madison's transcripts, the pages thwapping against one another in rapid succession as she crossed her legs and threw the thick folder dramatically down onto the Macallisters' ornate, gilded coffee table with the curved legs that made Phoebe feel like she was trapped in some awful, dusty museum surrounded by piles of hulking gold furniture with too many legs and the instant vertigo of crazily dipping crystal chandeliers. Come to think of it, Phoebe realized with a small smile as she looked around the cavernous living room, her random description fit the over-the-top opulence of the Macallisters' penthouse apartment to a T . . .

"But you girls need to get your act together—and quick."
Andrea frowned, her dark, bluntly cut chin-length bob swinging in the fading light coming in from the floor-to-ceiling windows, the tiny seed pearls adorning the neckline of her ivory cashmere Chanel sweater glinting in the soft glow of the chandelier overhead. "Because let me tell you—this lack of after-school commitments just isn't going to cut it at all."

Phoebe watched as Andrea blinked her spiky black lashes together rapidly and pursed her cranberry-colored, lightly glossed lips. Despite growing up somewhere in Queens, Andrea Cavalli had made a name for herself as first the admissions director at Princeton, and now as a private college admissions counselor to Manhattan's elite. Andrea was known for her scrupulous and creative methods in the college race, and boasted the highest placement rate at Ivies than any other professional college admissions counselor in the New York area, charging upwards of thirty thousand dollars for her services—which, to Phoebe's absolute dismay, often included preschool breakfast meetings and endless amounts of horrible *Bring It On*–esque cheerleader-type e-mails. Phoebe wasn't sure what was worse. Now that she and Jared were officially out in the open, all Phoebe really wanted to do was flirt with him on Facebook, leaving sexy posts on his all-too-crowded wall, and make out with him all night long. If she'd been seriously smitten before, she was *majorly* in lust now.

Phoebe glanced over at Madison, who was sitting sulkily at the other end of the couch, her arms crossed over her chest defiantly, and rolled her eyes sympathetically. Mad returned the look with a gaze that could stop a clock dead, rolling her green eyes so far up in her head that, for a minute, all Phoebe saw was the glaring whites of her friend's eyeballs. *Kill me,* Madison mouthed, her full lips perfectly reddened with YSL's Ruby Fix lip glaze.

Andrea leaned forward in her chair, shaking her hair from her face with an impatient toss of her head. "I'm going to lay my cards on the table—with no bullshit." Phoebe looked over at Mad, her jaw dropping slightly. "You girls can forget about getting into an Ivy unless you're willing to devote yourselves twenty-four hours a day, seven days a week to making your educational profiles exceedingly more viable."

"And how are we supposed to do *that*?" Mad snapped, crossing her toothpick-thin legs wrapped in ivory cashmere thigh-highs that peeked out from the hem of her minuscule black Dior skirt.

"By raising the level of your after-school commitments, for one," Andrea said with a tight smile that didn't quite hide her annoyance. She picked up both Madison's and Phoebe's academic folders and held them in one hand. "I mean, what do you girls *do* after school besides drink lattes and shop Fifth Avenue?"

There was a stunned moment of silence where Phoebe could almost hear the crickets in Central Park chirping busily. Phoebe looked over at Madison, who returned her gaze with a murderous look that positively screamed, *Who does this bitch think she* is? Oh, boy. Phoebe pushed her dark hair from her face and waited for the inevitable shit storm that was surely on its way via Madison's barbed tongue. But before Mad could open her mouth, Andrea rushed on, throwing the folders back onto the table with a decisive flick of her wrist.

"But that's all a thing of the past," Andrea said, the tone of her voice suggesting that she was really getting down to business. "I've arranged for you girls to spend two afternoons a week volunteering at Lenox Hill Hospital as candy stripers."

Phoebe's eyes glazed over as Madison made a sound that was somewhere between a gurgle and a scream. Bedpans and sick people? This woman had to be kidding. So. Not. Sexy. There was *no way* she was spending her afternoons in some smelly hospital, plumping pillows and waiting on old fogies when she could be rolling around in a king-sized bed with Jared. After all, she had her priorities to think about . . . and making out with her hot boyfriend was definitely at the top of the list.

And candy striping? Please. The only *stripping* she was going to be doing would be taking place in the privacy of her own bedroom. *Well,* Phoebe thought with a sigh that came from somewhere so deep in her chest that it felt like she was exhaling her very soul, *maybe the outfits will at least be cute.* Phoebe's brain flooded with images of Jared supine in bed, his bare, tawny skin in high relief against the white sheets. Of course, she'd be wearing the most adorable white nurse's uniform with a hem that stopped at her thighs as she bent over and wiped the sweat from his brow, the muscles in his biceps flexing as he pulled her to him and . . .

Just as Madison began babbling strenuously in protest and Phoebe became lost in her Florence Nightingale/Playboy Channel daydreams, Phoebe's phone began buzzing frantically from within the confines of her crimson Kate Spade purse. Ever since she'd picked up a new BlackBerry Storm a few days ago, the damn thing buzzed and alerted her practically every five minutes. Phoebe scrolled through her messages, then logged on to MySpace, her fingers screeching to a halt as she saw Drew's message. Phoebe frowned, her usually placid brow creasing like a linen dress on a humid day. It wasn't like she and Drew were exactly mortal enemies or anything, but it wasn't like they hung out every day outside of school either—or had anything in common besides the fact that their parents were currently fucking each other's brains out.

Wait . . . did Drew *know*?

Phoebe's mouth dropped open as she pondered the idea. She hadn't thought about it before, but now that he'd messaged her out of the blue, it made total sense. Maybe they *should* get together and talk this thing out. Actually, it might actually be nice to talk to someone who really *understood* what she was going through for a change. Whenever she tried to talk to Jared about how screwed up her family was, or about how lonely and lost she'd been feeling since her dad moved out, his blue eyes usually glazed over halfway through the conversation, which inevitably concluded with Jared trying to unhook her bra, unlace her boots, or distract her with some other dumbass, completely exasperating but hot, boy-type nonsense . . .

Phoebe's dark eyes widened as she read, thankful that Madison was now thoroughly engrossed with attempting to verbally eviscerate Andrea. If Phoebe was going to make this work, she was going to have to reply as quickly as she could before Madison got the heads-up, got interested, and grabbed the phone from her hands the way she usually did when whoever was around wasn't paying attention to her.

"And my *Dior*," Madison was practically yelling at Andrea, "it might pick up a staph infection. I mean, the fabric is so delicate that it might as well be human *skin*!"

Phoebe watched, half-amused as Andrea's eyes narrowed to slits and her inner Queens girl threatened to pounce. Phoebe was actually so engrossed in the drama unfolding—formidable competition that Andrea was turning out to be—that she almost forgot about the whole text messaging thing. But as Madison continued to yell, promising that any readily communicable diseases she might pick up if forced into candy striping would be coughed and sneezed continually in Andrea's direction until she undoubtedly became sick herself, Phoebe remembered Drew's plea, and bent her head over her phone. Her fingers deliberately pressed against the touch screen, realizing there was no way Mad could ever find out without consequences so severe that Phoebe might end up in the hospital herself. Or, she could always claim amnesia . . .

Phoebe smiled as she pressed SEND with the tip of her fingernail, and switched her phone to silent.

Hey, D.

Random is right. Hook up with me at UG at 7 if you want to talk . . .

L8tr,

P.

i'm dreaming of a green christmas . . .

"Phyllis, darling!" Melissa Von Norton strode into the St. Johns' living room as if she owned the place, the ice-pick heels on her chocolate brown, patent leather Manolo pumps noise-less on the deep pile of crimson-and-beige Oriental rugs that were strewn across the glossy wood floors, her camel colored shearling coat trailing behind her like an expensive, supple flag. "So lovely to see you again!" Melissa exclaimed, her low, mellifluous voice full of warmth as she pulled off her gold Michael Kors sunglasses and embraced Sophie's mother, who stood there stiffly, her hands coming to rest loosely on Melissa's back as if she was patting a delicate baby bird—not hugging one of the biggest movie stars on the entire planet.

"You," Melissa went on as soon as they'd pulled back from

one another, pointing one beige nail at Phyllis's chest, "are looking positively *stunning*." Melissa cocked her head to the side and flashed her trademark mega-watt smile that earned her upward of twenty million a film, her slightly almond-shaped blue eyes traveling down to take in Phyllis St. John's lithe figure beneath a discreetly patterned gray-and-white Diane von Furstenberg wrap dress. "Pilates?" she inquired, raising one delicately arched blond brow.

Phyllis blushed with pleasure, her sculpted cheekbones flushing in a way that made her suddenly appear much younger than her chronological age of forty. "Stripper Aerobics, actually," she said almost apologetically, taking Melissa by the arm and leading her over to the deep brown leather sofa.

"Wow," Melissa said, impressed, as she pulled off her coat to reveal a bronze silk shirt tucked into a pair of dark-washed True Religion jeans with yellow stitching, a Chanel belt cinching her tiny waist with a web of fine gold interlocking double C's. "Well, I've got to tell you, Phyllis—it looks like it's *definitely* working," she purred, laughing softly as she pushed her honey-colored mane back from her pale skin, which shone like it was exfoliated with diamonds on an hourly basis.

Sophie sank down into an overstuffed armchair grumpily, crossing her bare legs, which peeked out from a pair of magenta Juicy Couture shorts, and began obsessively pulling at the strings of her matching hoodie, wondering if anyone was going to even acknowledge her existence, much less perform routine social niceties like saying hello. Just as she was contemplating stomping off to her room and blasting Jay-Z until the chandeliers shook, Melissa's bottle-green eyes caught her own and held them, her lips curving softly into a smile. And all at once what Sophie found herself wanting more than anything in the world was to get to know this woman who had given birth to her, to find out who she really was, to be, in some way, a *real* part of her life. The feeling swelled up in her chest like a balloon full of hot air, and before she could help herself she was grinning back at her mother, her annoyance both forgiven and forgotten.

"Sophie, love," Melissa said, her blue, expertly lined eyes roaming over her daughter's face like she was trying to commit it to memory. Sophie couldn't help noticing that as soon as the word *love* left her mother's lips Phyllis flinched slightly in shock, her body recoiling from the word as if it were poison. "I wanted to speak with your . . . mother about what we discussed yesterday."

"Yesterday?" Phyllis wondered aloud, an edge of panic creeping into her usually carefully modulated voice. "When did you . . ." Phyllis began as she looked from Sophie back to Melissa, confusion spreading thickly across her face like a heaping spatula of Crème de la Mer. Sophie felt the hairs on her arms begin to stand at attention apprehensively as her mother's voice trailed off into nothingness.

"I surprised Sophie before school," Melissa said gaily, waving her hand languidly in the air as if it were no big deal. "And I asked if she might be willing to spend Christmas with me in Los Angeles."

There was a long silence. Sophie could hear the antique

Swiss clock ticking on the end table and the sound her breath made as it moved raggedly in her chest as she watched emotions shift and move across Phyllis's face like an incoming monsoon.

"Christmas is . . . a very important holiday in our household," Phyllis said, clearly struggling to retain her composure, and trying her best to choose her words carefully. "A *family* holiday," she finished decisively. Now it was Melissa's turn to flinch. Her face paled noticeably, the blood rushing away from her features. Sophie shifted uncomfortably on her chair, sticking her hands underneath the sleeves of her hoodie and running her fingers over her scars for reassurance. Watching this scene play out between her two mommies was beginning to resemble absolute torture. Until things really got ironed out, all this mother/daughter stuff was undoubtedly just going to be uncomfortable—full stop.

"I realize that," Melissa said slowly, carefully. "And my intention isn't to take Sophie away from you during the holidays. I thought we might be able to come to some sort of compromise." Melissa took a deep breath before continuing. "I've missed sixteen Christmases with Sophie, and I'd absolutely *hate* to miss another."

"I see," Phyllis said icily, looking down at her knees covered in sheer black stockings. Sophie couldn't help but notice the strained expression on her mother's face, the way her usually relaxed, lightly bronzed figure was pulled taut and tight, her hands clenched into fists at her sides. The currents of jealously between the two women felt like a thick, noxious smog that was almost stifling in its intensity. "Well, what did you have in mind?" Phyllis asked, her voice strained.

"I was thinking that Sophie could fly out late on Christmas Day," Melissa said evenly. "That way she could be with her . . ." Melissa said, clearly struggling for the right words, and trying desperately not to offend Phyllis in the arduous process, "well, *you*, on Christmas Eve—and *most* of Christmas Day. I was hoping she could stay with me for two weeks, but, of course, that's entirely your decision."

"Two weeks is out of the question," Phyllis said crisply. "We're taking our annual holiday trip to Aspen in January and I wouldn't want Sophie to miss it."

"Then how about a week?" Sophie asked tentatively, feeling like if she didn't manage to break into the conversation it was more than a distinct possibility she might scream—or hurl herself through the glass coffee table in sheer frustration. Sophie watched as Phyllis turned the idea around in her head, searching for a reason to say no. Just watching the obvious turmoil plastered all over the face of the woman who'd raised her made Sophie feel like she was about to lose it herself. She was definitely caught in the middle—and she had the sneaking suspicion that, no matter which way things went today, it wouldn't be the last time. There had to be something she could do or say to make this whole idea easier on everyone.

"Mom," she said softly, holding Phyllis's dark eyes with her own. "You've had me every Christmas for the last sixteen years. Melissa just wants to get to know me a little. You're not going to lose me or anything—I *promise*."

"*Exactly,*" Melissa said, chiming in, clearly relieved as she placed one hand on Phyllis's arm and patted her softly, like an infant she was trying to placate. "Sophie is *your* daughter. I'd just like to spend a little time with her."

Phyllis nodded, dabbing at the corners of her slightly reddened eyes with her fingers before she spoke, careful not to smear her dark gray liner. "Well, I suppose it's obvious that I don't like the idea . . ." With those words, Sophie's stomach dropped a distance of what felt like fifty feet, disappointment flooding her body like water. "But I think I'm outnumbered here," Phyllis continued with a grim smile.

Sophie's heart leapt in her body in a combination of relief and gladness, the disappointment suddenly banished. Before she could help it, she found herself grinning widely, her face stretching like taffy, hoping that Phyllis would smile back and let her know that everything was now all right. But instead, Phyllis reached over to the coffee table and picked up her untouched tea, cupping the paper-thin Mikasa china between her palms, and cleared her throat, suddenly all business again. Sophie had seen this kind of behavior before—more than once. Any kind of emotional outburst always made Phyllis feel exposed and vulnerable—so much so that she usually overcorrected the situation by immediately sealing off whatever emotion might bubble to the surface, and smothering it under a blanket of niceties and politesse.

"Sophie may leave the day *after* Christmas and stay for approximately one week," Phyllis said, her voice smooth and even now, her dark eyes blinking rapidly under her thickly lashed eyes. "But no more than that, for now."

"Agreed." Melissa nodded, clearly satisfied with the arrangement. "We'll take it slow," she agreed. "Baby steps."

"Baby steps," Sophie echoed, nearly beside herself with excitement, smiling happily at Melissa, but all of a sudden overcome with a wave of love for Phyllis. *This must be so hard for her*, Sophie thought, watching as her mother smoothed back her dark jaw-length hair, struggling to stuff her emotions away and act normal. *Maybe even harder than keeping it a secret for all of these years . . .*

"So, I will make all the travel arrangements." Melissa stood up, sliding her sunglasses back over her face. "And of course I'll send a car for her at the airport."

Sophie sat there barely hearing a word, the high-pitched voices that rose and fell like the dipping of bird wings in midflight mixed together pleasantly as she felt her face breaking into a smile so big she thought her cheeks might split open entirely, spilling the sparkly fairy dust of her happiness across the length of the room.

It was really going to happen—she was going to spend a whole week sitting down to breakfast with Melissa each morning, swimming laps beside her in the pool, and, of course, shopping Rodeo, bulging shopping bags from Kitson and Fred Segal slung over their shoulders, their identical blond heads tilted close together as they laughed at some private joke that only they understood, vanilla cupcakes from Sprinkles in their hands. Plus, she could visit the *original* Pinkberry, not to mention Les Deux! Maybe Melissa would even introduce her to Heidi and Spencer . . . It was all going to be so perfect that Sophie could barely contain her excitement.

As she got up to say good-bye, and Melissa's arms wrapped around Sophie briefly, gold bracelets jangling, her exceedingly floral perfume that smelled of roses and jasmine engulfing her like a wave, Sophie knew she was probably idealizing the trip, her mother, Hollywood—everything. But even if she *was* currently living in some kind of deluded slumberland, Sophie also knew that she didn't ever want to wake up . . .

secrets and lies

Casey stood nervously outside the pair of ornately carved mahogany doors that led to the Macallisters' penthouse apartment, the brass fixtures and knob polished to a blinding sheen, her pulse thudding out of rhythm in her veins, her heart skipping in her chest like flat rocks skidding across the surface of the boat pond in Central Park. She looked down at her faded Seven jeans and Gap red-and-navy tartan wool jacket that tied at the waist, and tried to quiet her breathing and stop the beads of sweat that were, even now, in danger of popping up on her forehead. This was ridiculous—she was as wracked with nerves as if she'd been granted a visitation with the Queen of England. Madison Macallister may not have ruled the British Isles as of yet, but she certainly dominated the entire Upper East Side—if not the whole impossibly tiny island of Manhattan—with a bling-encrusted fist. That being said, the last thing Casey wanted was to show up wearing anything that might cause Her Royal Crankiness to slam the door in her face as quickly as she'd opened it.

All afternoon she'd replayed the scene at lunch—Drew's weird, nervous behavior, so different from the playful quips she'd grown accustomed to, the kind he'd entertained them with in Central Park when she'd laid eyes on him for the first time in all his red-eyed, jet-lagged scrumptiousness. When he'd asked if he could call her, just before walking away, it had taken all of her willpower not to scream out, "Yes!" at the top of her lungs, then tackle him to the floor, ripping off his stupid sweater in the process. The problem was, the longer they didn't talk, and the more time she found herself spending with Darin, the more unsure she became about what she really wanted at all.

Casey took a deep breath, pressed the gold buzzer to the right of the door frame, relieved for once that the film crew was off presumably making someone *else* famous for fifteen minutes, and shook her hair out one last time before the door swung open. Mad stood there wearing a short, black A-line skirt and ivory cashmere thigh-highs, her feet encased in black patent leather Tory Burch ballet flats, her slim torso swaddled in a black cashmere top that wrapped around her body enticingly. Casey realized with no small degree of horror that as over the top as the outfit was, it was probably Madison's idea of after-school clothes—that is, if after-school activities took place at Pangea, Goldbar, or Bungalow—which, Casey knew all too well, wasn't exactly out of the question where Madison Macallister was concerned . . .

Madison smiled brilliantly, her teeth blinding next to her darkened hair. Casey still wasn't used to Mad's new look. It wasn't that she looked bad—far from it. Madison Macallister could wear a bag over her head and still be so gorgeous that total strangers would follow her down the street, barking like dogs and making obscene gestures with their hands. Her hair, now the color of the deliciously sinful, pudding-rich hot chocolate at Jacques Torres, just made her look less like *herself*— whoever that was—and more like Sarah Michelle Gellar in *Cruel Intentions*, which, come to think of it, was basically Mad's life story anyway . . .

"Casey!" Madison said triumphantly, opening the door wide so that the Macallisters' opulent Louis XIV–style foyer was revealed in all of its hushed, impeccably gold-leafed splendor. "I'm *so* glad you could make it!"

Huh? Casey felt like she was dreaming as she followed Madison through the entryway in a complete and utter daze. She couldn't help but wonder who the hell had kidnapped Madison Macallister and left this paradigm of niceness and virtue in her place. This had to be some kind of a joke. From the minute she'd moved into The Bram, Casey had always felt like Madison had been just barely *tolerating* her presence. Now here she was inviting her over, all smiles. It was definitely weird.

You have now entered The Twilight Zone, Casey monotoned to herself as she tried to suppress the fit of giggles that was threatening to bubble up in her throat as she took in the gilded fixtures, the amazing French doors just off the living room, the imported gray Italian marble floors, and the gently swaying crystal chandeliers that seemed to hang in every room. Wow. And double wow. The air in the penthouse even smelled different from the rest of The Bram—like a combination of lilies of the valley and fresh white sheets sprayed with lavender and dried in the hot sun. It made Casey want to curl up right there on the marble floor and take a big nap . . .

"I just got back from Phoebe's—my mom arranged for me to work with that college admissions counselor." Madison made a gagging noise, as if the very thought made her physically sick.

"So, how was it?" Casey couldn't believe it. Mad was actually making small talk with her!

"The very *definition* of purgatory," Madison groaned, shaking her hair out with a brisk shake of her head. "My room's through here," Madison called over her shoulder as they navigated the Macallisters' labyrinth of an apartment, her voice so light and innocuous without any traces of her trademark Madison bitchiness that Casey wondered again if she was in the right place. *Hey*, she wanted to say, *you do know that it's* me, *right? Casey McCloy? The girl you usually, ummm, can't* stand? She followed Mad into her room and closed the door behind them.

Casey blinked rapidly as she surveyed the private lair of the Upper East Side's reigning princess. Mad's ultramodern bedroom couldn't have been more different from the gilded excess of the rest of the apartment, with its chrome bed covered by a fluffy white Siberian goose down comforter, a modern white desk in the corner with chrome legs, and shiny hardwood floors the color of ripened honey. The ceiling above was painted the lightest sky blue, the color glazed, as if it had only been left to dry minutes before. Standing in the middle of all that white and blue made Casey feel as if she were standing on a cloud on a brilliantly bright day, the sun shining warmly on her face.

Mad sat down on the king-sized bed and patted the space next to her, indicating that Casey should follow. Casey took a deep breath and tried her best to act like sitting on Mad's bed with her was the most natural thing in the world, instead of the weirdest. She kicked off the pair of navy Tod's loafers she'd borrowed from Sophie last week that were just the teensiest bit too big, and sat down on the bed, crossing her legs beneath her. Madison toyed with a lock of her hair that was currently held back from her feline face by an ivory satin headband, and looked over at Casey, her green eyes quietly glittering.

"So . . ." Mad began slowly, "I kind of wanted to talk to you about Drew."

Casey's heart stopped dead in her chest. In the momentary lull, she imagined smacking herself vigorously on the sternum in order to revive her failing heartbeat like some crazed paramedic on one of those *Rescue 911*–type shows Nanna was so addicted to. Ever since Drew's welcome-home party at the beginning of the year when Mad had called her out in front of the entire Upper East Side and make her look the fool, Casey had been positively dreading this moment and simultaneously hoping they could somehow clear the air between them and start all over again. Casey swallowed hard and tried to think of what to say, but no matter how many different possibilities she turned over in her brain, none of them seemed likely to make it to her mouth.

"There's . . . some stuff going on that I think you should know about," Mad said carefully, her voice low and measured. She looked down and to the side, the sharp sweep of her perfectly applied black eyeliner clearly visible above her lash line. "I mean, *I'd* want to know if I were you."

"Like what?" Casey asked nervously, her voice wavering a little, despite her achingly deep desire to come off as cool and collected as possible. God, first her heart had come to a dead stop, and now it felt like it was trying to find a way out of her chest through her *mouth. Get up and leave!* Her inner pragmatist screamed. *Don't sit here and let her tell you something that's just going to make you feel bad! Why give her that satisfaction?*

Good point, Casey thought, her brow wrinkled in equal parts thought and horrified anticipation. *But what if she's just looking out for me? She invited me over here, didn't she? Maybe we're finally going to be friends . . .*

You are so deluded, her inner pragmatist intoned smugly. *Since when does Madison Macallister care about anyone else but* herself?

Before Casey could come up with a convincing reason as to why her inner pragmatist was wrong this time around, Madison cut off her train of thought and began to speak. "I met Drew at Space a few nights ago—he said he wanted to talk." Madison took a deep breath and looked Casey square in the face. "We ended up back at his place, and, well . . . things just kind of *happened*."

Now instead of feeling like her heart was about to stop completely or explode, a wave of coldness ran through Casey's body, a feeling so intense that she almost, just for a second, thought she might throw up all over Madison's pristine white rug.

"Was that the first time you guys . . ." Casey's voice trailed off. She was unable to bring herself to finish the sentence. *Jesus Christ*, she thought, feeling her cheeks flush brightly red with horror and embarrassment, the cold rapidly replaced with heat. *I'm sitting in a penthouse talking to Madison Macallister about her sex life. What's wrong with this picture?* And if that wasn't bad enough, the sex in question just happened to be with the boy she couldn't seem to stop thinking about—no matter what he did.

Madison's steely green gaze softened momentarily and she looked away. As bad as Casey felt, Mad suddenly looked even worse. She dropped her head and bit her bottom lip, her usually smooth, expressionless face suddenly reddened. "Not . . . exactly. And then the other night after we'd . . . well, he just kind of shut down in typical Drew fashion and I stormed out. He never even called me afterward, if you can believe that. And then, well, you saw the way he acted at lunch today! I totally wanted to call the moron police and have him cited for reckless abandonment."

"Macking and running?" Casey said, forcing herself to crack a joke, if only to hide how bad she actually felt.

"Definitely," Madison snapped, recovering her edge and reaching up to smooth her already glossy hair. "He's *such* a player." Madison's eyes were hard now, the glimpse of vulnerability that had risen so briefly to the surface now hidden behind a wave of anger.

As confused and horrible as she felt, Casey couldn't help but take comfort in the fact that she wasn't the only one getting the shaft from Drew. Well, not *literally* in her case. It was kind of comforting to realize that not even the Madison Macallisters of the world were safe from this kind of boy-induced heartbreak and confusion. If Drew was capable of treating Madison so callously, maybe the fact that they really hadn't said more than ten words to one another since Sophie's party meant she was better off without him . . . But if that was true, then why didn't she *feel* better off?

Casey sighed, wondering what to say next. Should she commiserate? Offer to take Mad to brunch on Sunday? Brush her hair? Start sobbing uncontrollably? All Casey knew was that despite the bomb Mad had just dropped, she didn't feel lucky—she just felt tired, not to mention completely emotionally deflated. As hard as she tried, she just couldn't seem to wrap her head around it: How could Drew just go back to Madison like he and Casey had never even been together at all? Well, maybe in his mind, they hadn't . . . Casey wasn't sure which thought made her feel more hopeless. It was clearly a tie.

"I just thought you should probably know," Mad said,

fully recovered. "I mean, I know you're with Darin now, but if you were thinking about getting back with Drew . . ."

"I'm not *with* Darin," Casey said exasperatedly, unable to keep the irritation from her voice. "I mean, I don't really know what's going on, but we're not, like, a *thing*. At least I don't think so . . ."

"You sound really sure about that," Madison mused with a small smile, reaching up and pulling her headband off, running one hand through her hair. Casey smiled weakly, still feeling a bit like her stomach was going to leap out of her body and project its murky contents all over the floor. "Anyway," Madison said, waving one pearly pink manicured hand in the air like she was chasing away a pesky insect, "I'm definitely cutting him off. I mean, how could I *not*?"

"I guess . . . I should, too," Casey mused, feeling like every word was sealing her doom. But how could she really give any other answer? Casey was jolted out of her convoluted thoughts as her cell phone began to buzz frantically. When she pulled it from her coat with an apologetic smile and stared at the tiny, glowing screen, her pulse quickened like she'd just been zapped with a cattle prod when she saw Drew's name illuminated.

"Who is it?" Mad said with annoyance, reaching out to grab the phone from Casey's hand.

"It's just my mom," Casey said quickly, hitting the ignore button with her thumb and sliding the phone back into her pocket before Madison could get her paws wrapped around it. Now she was really turning into a cardiac patient. Could seventeen-year-olds have heart attacks? Casey looked back at Mad, who had grabbed a nail file from her bedside table, and was now furiously shaping her already perfect nails.

"Want me to do yours next?" she asked without looking up.

"I'm not really a nail polish kind of girl," Casey said weakly, holding out her hands in front of her and surveying her horribly bitten nails, fingers splayed.

"Ugh," Mad said, looking up briefly and taking in Casey's chewed fingers. "We'll definitely have to do something about *that*." Madison reached beneath the bed and pulled out a chrome basket full of Chanel, YSL, Hard Candy, Essie, and Dior polishes, and threw them down on the bed between them. "Pick," she commanded, waving her file in the air like stabbing Casey for noncompliance was a distinct possibility.

Casey pawed through the cornucopia of polishes, the glass bottles slick beneath her sweaty fingers. It was totally surreal— not only was Madison confiding in her, but she was going to *do her nails*! This is what she'd wanted ever since she'd moved to New York, to fit in, to really feel like she belonged. Maybe they could somehow learn to put this whole Drew thing behind them and become real friends . . . But Casey couldn't help but wonder if the price was just too high. She just wasn't sure that she *wanted* to put Drew behind her—or if she was really capable of turning her back on him, and giving up on the idea that they'd ever be able to get back together again.

At least maybe not yet . . .

coffee . . . date?

Drew stirred an obscene amount of cream into the cup of hot black coffee on the table in front of him, watching as the inky black liquid turned the color of wet sand, and warmed his hands around the chipped porcelain cup. With everything that had been going on lately, Uncommon Grounds was one of the few places that felt like home anymore, that made him feel like he belonged in the plant-filled room, sitting in the familiar cracked red leather booths in front of the plate glass windows, and resting his elbows on the slightly greasy Formica tabletop.

As much like home as the comfortingly dilapidated café felt, his reasons for being there that day were totally, completely surreal, making him more than a bit nervous. Drew was certain that Phoebe was very practiced at this type of thing—meeting up with Madison or Sophie to drink concoctions of coffee, sugar, milk, and whipped cream with long-winded names and talk about the sex lives of friends and enemies alike, Drew's own name probably having popped up a fair number of times.

But even with all of her practice, Drew had a feeling that Phoebe would be a bit out of her element as well. These were their *parents'* sex lives they were going to be talking about, and just the very thought of that topic, of having the words *parents* and *sex* in such close proximity made Drew feel a little queasy. Weren't parents supposed to stop having complicated, not to mention illicit, sex lives *after* having children? Weren't they supposed to stop having sex at all, full stop? It was extremely uncool that his had continued to do so. Drew could only imagine the amount of psychotherapy he would need down the road in order to deal with it. And on top of everything, the whole thing was making him realize that wanting to be just like Woody Allen was a really bad idea, which just made him more pissed off. That *this* was the way that his life would resemble the films he loved was making him consider the possibility of picking a new favorite director, a fact that would tell anyone who knew him well that Drew was in way over his head.

Drew looked up from his cup just as Phoebe walked in the front door, bringing a cool blast of winter air along with her. Phoebe was dressed in a red-and-black plaid skirt, black tights, and a white dress shirt under a black wool vest. The entire ensemble made her look like a Young Republican as imagined by Anna Wintour.

"Hey, Pheebs," Drew said as she walked toward the table. "Been hanging out with the Pro-Lifers or something? You're looking very Red State chic in that getup."

"Which state is the red one?" Phoebe said with a look of confusion and she slumped down in the chair across from Drew, throwing a black bag into the booth next to her—a bag so huge and unwieldy that Drew wouldn't have been surprised to find a small child nestled within its voluminous folds.

"Never mind," Drew said, laughing slightly to himself. "Where'd you come here from?"

"A meeting with the Nazi college counselor that my mom hired." Phoebe pushed her mass of dark, silky straight hair off her shoulders with a grimace, her pale cheeks flushed from the cold air. "No matter how many times I see her, she insists on spending the first half hour telling me that I should've been making plans for college since I was practically in diapers. She should see the outfits I was wearing then—those zip-up jersey cat suits with the hood and the sewed-on socks were hideous. How was I supposed to be making decisions about college when I was clearly incapable of putting an *outfit* together? Not to mention the fact that at the time I wanted to be Rainbow-fucking-Brite when I grew up. I can't believe my mother actually *pays* this woman."

"Wow," Drew said, sipping his coffee and smiling at Phoebe's rage. "Sounds like a nightmare. So what does she do? Read drafts of your college essays and stuff?"

"Ha. If it were only that simple," Phoebe said with a snort. "It's more like she reads my *life* like it's an essay, making and enforcing any changes she damn well pleases. It's worse than having a mother, believe me. It's like she wants to build a brand-new, Ivy League Admissions Counselor–friendly Phoebe robot, and another robot named Madison with the exact same reading list and extracurricular activities."

"Madison is in on this thing?" Drew asked, his stomach doing a strange, quick jump followed by a long, slow roll upon hearing her name, his caffeine-shaky hands quickly coating with a fine, cold film of sweat.

"Yeah, uh, I guess my mother got her mom convinced of this woman's cloning powers or whatever. But we don't have to talk about that if you don't want to," Phoebe said quickly, as the waitress walked over, pencil stuck behind her ear like wooden jewelry.

"I'll just have a latte," Phoebe said as the waitress hovered expectantly before stomping busily away. That was one of the things Drew loved about this place. There was no ass-kissing at Uncommon Grounds. It reminded him of the coffee shops downtown that he used to hang out in for hours before his parents moved to the Upper East Side—otherwise known as the robot factory.

"Why would I have any problem talking about Madison," Drew said defensively as soon as the waitress became vapor, crossing his arms over his favorite navy Triple Five Soul hoodie with the ink stains on the right sleeve. "You can talk about her all you want."

"I just thought that, well, after lunch today . . ." Phoebe's voice trailed uncomfortably off. She looked down and immediately unwrapped her napkin and began playing obsessively with her silverware.

"Don't they want you to have, like, personality?" Drew said hurriedly, changing the subject before Phoebe had time to bring Madison back up again. "I always thought that admissions applications were about showing yourself as an individual, setting yourself apart from everyone else. Wouldn't being exactly the same as someone else on paper actually *hurt* your chances of getting in?"

Phoebe let Drew's rudeness slide, perhaps understanding his not wanting to talk about Mad and not wanting to have to admit to that fact. "If by showing your personality you mean the right amount of hours volunteered at all the right charities, then yes—college apps are all about personality," she said with an ironic smile. "But if by personality you mean expressing the emotional reaction you had to a Radiohead CD, then it's State Schoolville for you, Drewster."

"Not like anyone would care at this point. My parents are apparently too busy fucking strangers to pay much attention to me and my future," Drew said bitterly, momentarily forgetting that "strangers" just happened to include Phoebe's mother. Whoops. Open mouth, insert Puma. He probably could've handled that a lot more gracefully, much like everything else in his train wreck of a life.

"Hey now," Phoebe said, "I don't think my mom exactly counts as a stranger. And count yourself lucky—my mom manages to find the time to sleep around *and* continually harass me about college at the same time. At least you're getting *something* out of your dad's cheating."

"So . . ." Drew said slowly, unsure how he actually felt about saying the dreaded words aloud, "I guess you heard."

Phoebe nodded, dipping her head down mid-nod and keeping it there, her eyes focused on the swirly pattern on the Formica tabletop.

"The way he explains it, it's not cheating. He and my mom have an *understanding*." Drew picked up his cup and took a greedy sip of lukewarm coffee, wanting the caffeine rush. "What kind of bullshit is that? An understanding? This isn't the 'Modern Love' column in the Sunday *New York Times*. Parents are supposed to be responsible and put together and preferably not screwing *other* people's parents. Isn't getting married and having kids a way of saying that you're *done* sleeping around? Don't you have to admit that to yourself to even go through with it?"

"In a perfect world, I'd say, yes, definitely," Phoebe responded carefully. "But in a perfect world, people who get married are in love with each other, and generally make each other happy. And when it comes to *my* parents, that's *definitely* not the case." The waitress sailed by, dumping Phoebe's latte on the edge of the table, foam sloshing over the edge of the glass. "You know," Phoebe mused, pulling her drink toward her and resting her hand on her chin, a thoughtful expression animating her delicate features, "if she wasn't my own mom, I probably wouldn't even blame her for it."

"How can you be so blasé? I mean, these are our *families* we're talking about, Pheebs." Drew pushed his coffee away out of frustration, the need to have something to do with his hands consuming every muscle on his lanky frame.

"I know," Phoebe said quietly, after a long pause, her eyes meeting Drew's and holding them. "Believe me, I'm aware of that. Did you hear that my dad's moved out?"

"No shit?" Drew said, unable to keep the surprise from his voice, and feeling immediately ashamed of the way he'd been acting. God, maybe Madison was right—he really *was* kind of an asshole sometimes. Things may have been less than perfect in the Van Allen household as of late, but at least there had been no talk of anyone moving out. Well, at least not that he knew of . . . "Wow, Pheebs," Drew said, swallowing hard, "I'm really sorry—I didn't know."

"Yeah, well," Phoebe said, her dark eyes filling with tears as she looked away and pretended to be fascinated with the bustle currently going on outside the window, her eyes scanning the busy sidewalks teeming with people, like her life depended on it.

"How's Bijoux taking it?" Drew asked gently, not sure what to say, or do, next. Everything he said seemed like a potential hot spot, or trap, and he was worried, as always, that without meaning to he would inevitably say or do the wrong thing.

Phoebe grabbed her napkin and wiped her nose, then looked away from the window, her eyes meeting Drew's again with a look that could only be described as angsty. In that moment, Drew couldn't help but notice how incredibly lovely

Phoebe was. Even with her red nose and rapidly reddening eyes, even with her face full of despair, or maybe because of it, her hair was dark and glossy, her skin so pale and luminous it seemed almost incandescent. Or maybe it was just the fluorescent lighting . . .

"I don't know," Phoebe muttered, taking a sip of her latte, her full red lips covered with foam before she licked it off with the tip of her pink tongue. "She's six, you know? She doesn't really *get* it. Beebs just runs around asking 'Where's Daddy, where's Daddy' all the time—and no one knows what to say to her. Including me. *Especially* me."

"That's got to be tough," Drew said, pushing his hair back with one hand. "Is there anything I can do to help you out? I mean, I know I've been a bit of a righteous asshole since you got here, up on my high horse about relationships and everything. I mean, do you want to, like, talk about it? I'm a pretty good listener when I really *try*."

"It's okay, Drew," Phoebe said, laughing a little, then glancing away before looking back at him, her dark eyes wet with moisture and mirth. "It was nice to just be able to tell someone that it happened. I think that's all I can really do right now—it's all too new and terrible to actually try to wrap my head around. But really, thanks for offering. It means a lot."

Drew felt another pang of intense attraction as Phoebe spoke. There was something about seeing a girl at a moment when she was totally vulnerable, her guard down, that had always fascinated Drew. It might happen in the midst of a heavy make-out session or at a more emotional moment like the one with Phoebe, but it was a time when he felt that he could really see the person for who they were. Sometimes, he was terrified of what he saw in girls when it happened, but seeing Pheebs be so totally open made Drew feel both curious and excited. He wanted to know that person he saw in those short few seconds. He wanted to make out with her and see if he could bring back that look again, to see if it would be the same. And if it wasn't, that'd be totally fine, because he really just wanted to make out with her. Kind of bad. *This is Phoebe,* he told himself. *Get a goddamn grip on yourself—she's practically your sister, not to mention the fact that she already* has *a boyfriend.* Well, Drew mused, trying to calm his racing pulse, it wasn't like Phoebe's mom didn't have a husband, but that hadn't exactly stopped Drew's dad or anything . . .

Drew smiled and lifted his cup of coffee. "Here's to getting all of our sleeping around out of the way *before* we get married," he said, trying to wipe all illicit thoughts from his brain and replace them with friendship and caffeine. Phoebe smiled and clinked the edge of her porcelain coffee mug against his. "And to be completely honest with you," Drew went on, a light flush running across his face, "I hope that between now and whenever I get married, that sleeping around and working out whatever shit I have to becomes a whole lot more about a good time and not the screwed-up emotional mess it's been so far."

Phoebe looked straight at him, smiling over the lip of her cup. "Sounds to me like maybe you've been sleeping with the wrong people."

guess who's coming to dinner . . .

"Madison, darling! We're all waiting!"

Madison shuddered as her mother's voice rang through the echoing space of the Macallisters' penthouse apartment, the low rumble of Antonio's voice layered directly underneath it like honeyed icing on a cake made of rocks and jagged pieces of broken glass. She was looking forward to this dinner about as much as a rectal exam performed with a whirring chainsaw— actually, the exam might even be preferable to the torture that currently awaited her at the dinner table. When the Pulse producers had called earlier, saying that they wanted to "drop in" for some final footage of a "typical" family dinner, Madison didn't have the heart to break it to them that the only tradition in the Macallister household was the regularity with which Edie downed her various cocktails and prescription drugs.

And once Edie found out that their evening meal was about to be immortalized on camera, she sprang into action—calling out to The London for takeout, which she then directed the maids to arrange artfully onto the Macallisters' own Spode plates so the food would look "authentically" homemade, and popping out for a quick blowout at Elizabeth Arden. Adding insult to injury was the fact that the pool boy—Madison's newest nickname for her mother's jailbait boyfriend—had, of course, been invited. Madison walked over to her full-length mirror, which took up most of one sparkling white wall, and freshened her lip gloss, running the wand of Chanel Glossimer in Spark over her already red, glossy lips, smacking them together loudly and making a kissy face, then sticking out her tongue at her own reflection and crossing her eyes hard until her image was replaced with absolute blackness.

As soon as she walked into the formal dining room—a room that was only used on special occasions—the brightness of the lights that Pulse had set up smacked her in the face like a wet towel. God, those fucking lights were so bright they were practically deafening . . . and what was worse was that they showed every little imperfection—not that she had many, but still, they made her nervous. It was about the equivalent of someone shrieking in your face for a good ten minutes without stopping. Melanie, the red-haired producer, hovered at the far end of the room, fussing with a pile of black, snakelike cords she was desperately trying to tame into submission.

Edie was seated at the table wearing a floor-length, black Valentino gown with wide gold stripes that she'd ordered from Paris in September after the fall collections premiered, her champagne blond mane tumbling artfully around her shoulders, a glass of vodka sweating in one hand, the ice cubes rattling against the fine crystal like tuneless music. A six-carat pink diamond that Madison's father had given her for their tenth wedding anniversary sparkled on her finger, winking in the candlelight like a mirage. Antonio stood behind her, leaning over the back of the chair to whisper in her ear, his lips inches away from her flesh. Just watching this spectacle made Madison's appetite run to Siberia—permanently.

"There you are!" Antonio intoned triumphantly, his voice more purr than exclamation. *"Cara,"* he said walking over to her, looking almost too gorgeous in a black Prada blazer with fine gray pinstripes, a dove gray dress shirt, and dark gray Gucci pants with a slim black alligator belt strung through the loops. "You look perfect—as usual." Madison tried not to grimace as he leaned in and kissed her on the cheek, the scratch of his stubble sandpapering her skin, his cologne enveloping her in a blanket of lemons and musk. Ugh, it was so annoying. Why did he have to still be hot? Why couldn't the very fact that he had ditched her for her own mother totally negate all possible thoughts of his hotness? In fact, why couldn't he be vaporized from planet Earth altogether, along with all the other guys she never wanted to ever lay eyes on again—or, at the very least, banished from the island of Manhattan . . .

"Madison, come and sit next to me," Edie said in her best Mother of the Year voice, holding her arms out in front of her. Madison rolled her eyes and disentangled herself from the Italian Stallion, glaring at him before walking over to the table and plopping ungracefully down in one of the crimson damask chairs that Edie had ordered from Paris, kicking the heel of her black ballet flats in time to the pounding in her head, and crossing her arms over her C cups. Why did just being in the same room as Edie and Antonio give her a massive migraine? *Migraine?* Madison thought silently, *yeah, right.* It was probably a goddamn brain tumor . . .

"Madison," Melanie yelled out, sounding totally exasperated, "we're going to start filming now, all right?" Melanie blew her curly red hair from her face, and pushed up the sleeves of her puke green American Apparel long-sleeved thermal tee.

"Whatever." Madison rolled her eyes, too annoyed and exhausted by the events of the past few days to really give a shit how she came across on film tonight. They'd probably edit everything to shreds anyway . . .

Antonio sat down next to Edie, resting his arm over the back of her chair. Like clockwork, they immediately began cooing and making disgusting baby noises at one another like a pair of complete and utterly mindless sex zombies. Ugh. Mad's stomach lurched toward her mouth. If she wasn't careful, she was going to hurl all over her mother's favorite lace tablecloth—the one that she'd had commissioned from a couple of nuns in some convent in Switzerland. Go figure.

"Madison," Edie began excitedly, "Antonio and I . . ." She reached over, taking Antonio's bronzed hand in her own, gazing adoringly up at his face as if he was personally responsible for sending the sun around the earth each day. "Well." Edie turned back to Madison and blushed girlishly, giggling. "We have something to tell you, dear. Big things are on the horizon!" she chirped in an irritatingly cheerful voice.

Perfect, Mad thought, leaning over the table and grabbing the frosty bottle of sauvignon blanc in the center of the table, pushing away the nauseating gargantuan floral arrangement of roses, Casablanca lilies, and freesia that made her feel like she was choking on toxic floral fumes, and poured herself a hefty glass. *Goddamn flowers,* she thought, swallowing wine like it was Evian, *sucking up all the goddamn oxygen in the room.* She'd heard this buildup before from Edie. It could only mean one thing—that ravioli boy was moving in. Well, if that happened there was just no way she was going to deal. She'd get an apartment at the Plaza before she'd ever agree to share the same living space with Edie and her Boy Wonder.

"Madison?" Edie inquired quasi-testily. Mad could tell that she really wanted to raise her eyebrows, however the Botox injections were definitely making it a no-go. "Did you *hear* me?"

"Loud and clear, *Mom,*" Madison snapped, refilling her glass to the tippy top this time, and raising it to her lips.

"Cara," Antonio said smoothly, his tanned face flickering in the glow from the lit ivory candles in the sterling silver candelabra placed on the cherrywood sideboard. "I have asked

your mother if she would do me the honor of becoming my wife."

Madison felt her wineglass slip through her fingers and heard it shatter against the polished parquet floor, the sound reverberating loudly in her ears. Maybe it was just the lights in her face, the camera that hovered across the room, but she *thought* she'd heard Antonio say that he had asked Edie to marry him. Madison looked down at the spilled wine, which was now rapidly forming a slick puddle at her feet. Clearly she was hallucinating—maybe she'd sprayed her Frederic Fekkai sculpting spray too close to her face this afternoon . . . Whatever the reason, this *had* to be some kind of misunderstanding—because if it *wasn't*, she was rapidly going to lose what was left of her fucking mind.

"And of course I accepted!" Edie squealed, leaning over and nuzzling Antonio's cheek with her overly powdered nose, blind to Madison's obvious shell shock. Edie turned back to her daughter, her face glowing in the candlelight. "So, we're thinking a June wedding, though that may not be enough time to book St. Patrick's or the Plaza, but I did meet the most fabulous wedding planner at that reception at the Waldorf last weekend, and I was thinking that maybe we could . . ."

Unable to stand even a moment more of this nonsense, Madison leapt from her seat, pushing her chair back so hard that it made a horrible scraping sound, probably gouging out large pieces of parquet. "You CANNOT be SERIOUS!" she screamed in a voice that sounded as though she was being strangled to death by a python. "You've only been divorced from dad for a year—not *even!*" Madison pointed at the sparkling diamond on Edie's left hand. "You're still wearing the ring, for God's sake!"

"Darling," her mother began in that tone of voice that Madison absolutely hated—the eminently oh-so-reasonable lilt that made her want to claw her own skin off. "I've spoken to your father, and he's all *for* it."

"Of COURSE he is," Madison yelled, her hands clenching into fists. "He's probably relieved not to have to pay your *Bergdorf's* bill anymore!"

Madison could feel the air moving faster and faster through her lungs, and her head began to feel light and dizzy, like it was about to become untethered from her neck and just pop off and begin floating across the room like a sick, bloated balloon. If this didn't just stop—if *everything* didn't stop, she was going to pass right the fuck out, face first into Edie's two-hundred-dollar flower arrangement, and *then* she was going to kill someone. Antonio as her *stepfather?* This was *so not happening.*

"Madison," Antonio said, getting up and pushing his chair back. "We were hoping you would be glad for us, no? Don't you want your mother to be happy?"

Madison paused, literally shaking with rage as she pondered the question. "NO!" Madison slammed her hand down on the table, causing the flower arrangement and the candles to shake precariously. "Why should I when obviously she doesn't care about *my* happiness. If she did she never would've divorced my father! And she *certainly* wouldn't be contemplating marrying some guy fifteen years her junior! You're *not*

Demi Moore, you know," Madison snapped, pointing an index finger in Edie's direction. "Even if you did fly all the way to Austria to have that revolting, leech-infested beauty torture."

A month ago, Edie had read an article crediting Moore's ageless good looks to a series of bizarre treatments she'd had done in Vienna, where live leeches were attached to her body and encouraged to bite in order to "detoxify the blood." Needless to say, Edie had booked a flight quicker than you could say "mental delusion." Edie's face drained of color, the skin turning the greenish white of a corpse. *She looks like a dead thing*, Madison thought as she watched her mother struggle to remain composed. *A corpse in a Valentino gown.*

"Madison, dear," Edie said carefully, pausing to gulp from her glass of wine, "I only want what's—"

"What's *best* for me?" Madison snapped, cutting her off before Edie could finish her thought. "Really, Mother," Madison said, her green eyes filling with frustration and tears, "you don't have the first *clue*." Madison looked around the room wildly, her green eyes unfocused with angry tears, remembering all too late that the cameras were in fact still there, the lens recording all of her epic family failures. Broken family with screwed up parental units wasn't the part she'd signed on to play when she'd agreed to this nightmare of a show. She was supposed to be perfect, goddammit! And that meant onscreen *and* off. It wasn't fair—the insulated, totally unreal world of television was supposed to be the *one place* where everything worked out perfectly at the end of the half hour . . . including her current mess of a life.

If she had to stay in that room for another moment, she'd either start full-out sobbing, become psychotically violent, or puke, and none of these options were, as far as she was concerned, even remotely acceptable. Madison bolted from the room, throwing her chair down as she went, the sound of the heavy wood and soft damask hitting the floor in a rush of air filling her with a fleeting moment of satisfaction. Madison swung the door to her room behind her roughly, relishing the sound of the wooden frame splintering under her ministrations, and sank to the floor, pulling her knees to her chest and hugging them with both arms, too angry and helpless to do anything other than begin to cry silently, her green eyes squinted shut, her head falling to her chest like a broken flower.

ménage à trois

"So, what are you up to this weekend?"

Darin Hollingsworth shook his shaggy black hair from his angular face, and pulled his Brooklyn Industries black bomber jacket closer to his skinny frame, wrapping his arms around his body as he kicked one red Converse high-top against the stone steps that lined the front of Meadowlark Academy. Casey looked over from her perch on the step adjacent, both waiting and wanting to feel the rush of butterflies she'd experienced the other night at Southpaw. But no matter how hard she concentrated, the only act her stomach was currently engaged in was digesting the half of a toasted poppy seed bagel she'd managed to wolf down this morning before running out the door to school.

Ever since she'd left Madison's last night, she'd been feeling totally confused. She'd lain in bed last night well past two A.M. watching the patterns the streetlights made glowing faintly yellow across the ceiling, the mournful sounds of Kate Walsh's *Clocktower Park* set to repeat on her iPod. If Mad honestly wanted to become friends, then Casey knew that she had to really try to put her feelings for Drew—whatever they were—out of her mind. *Darin's cool,* she told herself as Kate droned away in her ears. But no matter how many times she repeated the words in her head, she couldn't help but feel like she was trying to convince herself, to talk herself into feeling something that she didn't know if she actually felt for Darin. Still, what better way to try to distract herself from the whole Drew dilemma then by hanging out with the shaggy-haired, black-clad indie wonder? Except that it wasn't quite going as smoothly as she had imagined . . .

"I'm not sure," Casey said, trying to come off breezy and carefree, hoping simultaneously that he'd ask her out and drop the subject altogether. Casey stared out into the bustle of the street, sunlight blinding her gray eyes, the very last of the fall leaves skittering down the sidewalk, a dry, brown dance in a sudden gust of wind. It was one of those absolutely perfect winter days before the first snow blankets the sidewalks, before the freezing rain and gray patches of slippery ice. The air was bracingly cold and the sky a breathtakingly clear and perfect blue. The yellow awning of a Sabrett's hot dog cart glowed brightly in the sunlight, and the mouthwatering scent of grilled hot dogs and salt-encrusted hot pretzels made Casey's stomach begin to growl, reminding her that half a poppy seed bagel wasn't exactly rocket fuel.

Casey blew on the surface of her milky Earl Grey tea and wished she'd remembered to grab a sleeve so that she wouldn't be searing third-degree burns onto the skin of her palms. She was so nervous already from what she, ummm, *wasn't* feeling that she didn't think she could remotely stomach coffee this morning. "My mom's supposed to be coming into town this weekend, so I'll probably have to stick pretty close to home."

"Oh," Darin said, an obvious note of disappointment creeping into his voice. "That sucks. But I guess you'll be pretty glad to see her, right?" Darin reached into his dark gray Timbuk2 messenger bag covered with chipped buttons and peeling, brightly colored stickers of The Kills, Portishead, and The Strokes, and began rummaging around at the bottom, his face marked with concentration.

"Well, yes and no." Casey laughed, bringing her lips to the edge of the cup, then backing off when she felt the heat still radiating off the surface in waves. "I mean, don't get me wrong—I love her, you know? We just don't always get along." Casey shuffled her navy ballet flats against the stone, wondering why her conversations with Darin didn't have the same excitement, the same manic pull as her conversations with Drew, why she didn't feel a force field of static electricity crackling between their bodies, why blue sparks weren't showering the air between them. Was it just chemistry, the fact that her particular chromosomes and pheromones were hopelessly attracted to his? Casey exhaled, releasing a cloud of white smoke into the air and shivered beneath her kelly green cardigan and the Tommy Hilfiger black wool coat on which she'd spent all of her allowance for the next two months. Placing her cup carefully down on the steps, she wrapped her arms around her knees for extra warmth, her jeans doing little to alleviate the cold kiss of the stone steps on the backs of her legs.

"Yeah," Darin said, after a long pause, "it's not like my dad's going to win the award for Father of the Year anytime soon." Darin gave a short, uncomfortable laugh, pushing the hair from his face, his eyes flashing momentarily with unspoken anger.

Casey nodded, biting her bottom lip, racking her brain for something to say that might make Darin feel better, but coming up empty-handed. After all, it wasn't as if Barbara was such a stunning maternal presence either . . . Just then, Drew walked out of the front doors and started down the steps, a cup of coffee in one hand, dark sunglasses masking his face, wearing a black pea coat, a white-and-black boldly striped wool scarf swinging jauntily around his neck. At the sight of him, Casey felt her pulse begin thudding like a bass drum, her heartbeat abnormally loud in her ears. *Shit*, her inner dating Nazi lamented woefully. *Now he's going to think you're with Darin!*

Well, aren't *I?* Casey shot back silently, blushing and forcing herself to not only tear her gaze away from Drew's hotness, but to redirect her obvious lust to the boy sitting next to her. At the sight of Casey and Darin huddled together on the steps, Drew stopped in his tracks, his gaze beneath the dark shades seemingly locked on Casey, and exhaled heavily, resuming his trajectory down the stairs. *Was he looking at me,* Casey wondered, getting slightly hysterical as Drew approached. *And, more important, after what happened between him and Madison, do I still want him to look at me?*

Really, her inner dating Nazi said with no small degree of contempt. *Is that even a* question?

"What's up, guys?" Drew descended the steps, stopping at the bottom and turning to face Casey and Darin, doing that aggressive chin tilt that boys loved to use to punctuate a verbal greeting—or sometimes even in place of one.

"Mr. Van Allen," Darin said breaking into a grin, "what is UP?"

"Not much," Drew said, reaching out to slap hands with Darin, his dimples winking adorably in his lightly stubbled face as he smiled back, his dark, slightly messy hair shining in the sunlight. Casey watched Drew and Darin interact, fascinated as always by the bizarre, impossible to decipher boy code of meaningless questions and violent slaps guys routinely inflicted on one another. "What are you guys up to?"

"Just kicking it with Ms. McCloy here," Darin said, angling his head toward Casey.

"I see," Drew said, rocking back and forth from one foot to the other, a movement that Casey couldn't define as being either anxious or a step away from violence. It reminded Casey of her first day in New York, when she'd met Drew in the park while in the midst of being verbally patted on the shoulder and stabbed in the back by Madison Macallister—a routine she was now fully familiar with. At the time Drew had said something about observing the girls in their natural habitat, like they were wild animals. Sitting there on the steps, she felt more like she was watching male hyenas interact on some Discovery Channel or Animal Planet show than being with two of her boyfriends. Or, umm . . . friends that just happened to be boys.

"You got anything going on this weekend?" Darin asked, the same grin still on his face, his right foot tapping quickly and repetitively against the steps. "Any big plans?" Darin reached out and put one pale hand on Casey's knee, his skinny fingers curling around and squeezing tight. Casey flinched at his touch, quickly pulling her leg away from his territorial grip—one that she wasn't exactly certain he was entitled to. *But am I really the one who gets to decide,* she asked herself, feeling more and more like some arbitrary prize being silently battled for—but for the sake of the battle alone. She'd had just about enough of these safari wildlife politics that had suddenly popped onto these gray stone steps on a New York winter day, and she was just about to leave when her own animal instincts were aroused by the sound of Drew saying her name.

"I don't know. No big plans, really." Drew took a sip of his coffee, the steam fogging the lenses of his sunglasses almost immediately. "What about you, Casey?" Drew gestured with his cup in Casey's direction, the coffee sloshing dangerously close to the rim. "You have anything going on?"

Casey's boy-talk translation skills were becoming seriously overtaxed. She stared at Drew wordlessly, unable to decipher what he meant by the question, or think of anything to say in return. Did Drew just ask her to do something this weekend? Did he kind of sort of *maybe* ask her out on a *date*? Or was she just hopelessly deluded? The bigger question, of course, was why she even cared—Drew had slept with Madison less than a week ago. That should've put any speculation about what Drew was or *wasn't* asking completely to rest. But whatever he was up to, Casey couldn't help but notice that it had certainly gotten the butterflies in her stomach flapping their wings almost psychotically, giving Drew serious points against Darin in whatever game it was they all—herself now included—seemed to be playing.

"Uhhhhh . . ." Casey stalled, feeling at a loss as to how to form the correct response, wanting to make sure that she said all of the right things. She was starting to feel like she needed to give up on French and study boy-speak for her language requirement. It was amazing how nuanced and inane it could be at the *exact* same time. "I'm not sure yet," she managed to stammer, feeling disoriented by the fact that she couldn't see Drew's eyes behind the dark lenses he was wearing. Drew nodded his head slowly, contemplatively, then took a sip of his coffee. What was he thinking? Why were boys always such an unfathomable mystery?

"Cool," Drew said, nodding his head slowly.

"Yeah, sounds like everyone has an exciting weekend ahead," Darin said sarcastically, with a small, short laugh.

Drew pulled back the wool cuff of his coat, glancing at the chrome Tag Heuer on his wrist. "I've got to get to class, guys. I'll catch you two around," he said, hitching his messenger back up on his shoulder.

"Good call, my man," Darin replied, standing up from the steps, "I've got to run myself. Oh, and Drew, if nothing comes up for you this weekend, there's this new power-pop type-o-band from Brooklyn called Get to the Chopper playing out in Greenpoint if you want to check them out—I think I'm going to make the trek out there myself. They're supposed to be rad."

Casey looked on in disbelief, her mouth opening in a small, surprised O shape, as Drew walked away, his black-clad back getting smaller and smaller as he made his way down the curb and stopped at the hot dog cart, reaching into his back pocket and pulling out his wallet. Had this all ended with Darin and *Drew* making plans? Or was it just a front, a ruse—more passive-aggressive boy-battle bullshit. She had absolutely no idea. But she had gone from feeling that she figured into both boy's weekend plans to feeling pretty certain that it was going to be a weekend of *Law & Order* reruns and black-and-white cookies with Nanna for her.

slipping and falling

Drew grabbed Olivia Johansson's red mitten-clad hand, and tilted his head back, looking up at the enormous Christmas tree that towered over the ice rink at Rockefeller Center like a fragrant, benevolent angel, the colored lights adorning its wide-spread branches twinkling softly in the brisk night air as his feet glided smoothly across the slick, frozen surface of the rink. The rink was teeming with skaters wrapped in cashmere coats and puffy down jackets, wool hats pulled low over cold ears. At the far end of the rink, five or six young boys swaddled in enough winter clothing to kill a small child attempted a game of hockey, passing a black puck around the ice with their curved wooden sticks—much to the obvious dismay of the other skaters.

"I can't believe you've never been here!" Drew shouted over the syrupy rendition of "Oh Come All Ye Faithful" that was pumping gleefully through the large speakers that hung over the rink. "And you call yourself a New Yorker," he scoffed playfully with a half-smile, pulling Olivia behind him, her dark hair floating out in the air like a streamer the color of coffee grounds, her creamy cheeks flushed from the combination of the cold air and spinning around the ice. Here, in this place he'd loved ever since he was a kid, and with a pretty girl who wanted nothing from him but this date, this one moment (well, so far, at least), Drew felt himself relaxing for the first time in weeks, the tension ebbing away like ice melting in his limbs, defrosting the tight muscle of his heart. He'd always loved New York, and the city was never more magical than during the holiday season, when the whole place glittered like a sprawling, gaily wrapped package just waiting to be torn open and savored. Drew felt a twinge around his heart as he thought momentarily of Casey. When they were still seeing each other, he'd planned on taking her down Fifth Avenue just as soon as the lavish window displays were unveiled, knowing that she would find them as magical as he always did . . .

"Why stop here—why don't you take me to the Chrysler Building next?" Olivia joked, letting go of his hand briefly to adjust her matching red cashmere hat atop her head, giving him a wide smile that exposed rows of teeth that glowed with the serene luster of whitened ivory. "I mean, I haven't been there *either*."

"It's a date," Drew said lightly, turning around so that he

was skating backward, with Olivia facing him, taking her hands again in his own and holding on firmly. "Or we could get *really* touristy and check out the windows on Fifth before they take them down," Drew said with a chuckle.

Olivia laughed warmly, slipping a bit and grasping wildly in the air, then regaining her balance at the last moment, a look of palpable relief moving over her face. It was weird. Now that he thought about it, Olivia kind of looked a little like Phoebe . . . if Phoebe was inexplicably cloned in a pod along with a young Elizabeth Taylor . . . And speaking of Phoebe, Drew wasn't sure what kind of sparks had been flying between them last night at the coffee shop, but he did know that, whatever they were, it was a decidedly bad idea to even consider fanning them into a steady flame. But Drew *also* couldn't help noticing that, where girls were concerned, he seemed drawn to sticking his hand in the fire every chance he got.

When Drew had called Olivia after school and suggested night skating at the infamous rink just off Columbus Circle, Olivia had groaned forebodingly, her voice both sarcastic and self-effacing. "I'm hopeless," she'd warned. "You'll probably regret it after five minutes on the ice with me—I haven't skated since I was ten, and I pretty much sucked back then, too." She laughed, the sound reminding him of bells, of a crystal chandelier tinkling in the breeze. And even before he hung up, he knew that he was in all kinds of trouble. First of all, there was the whole high school issue—namely, that he attended one. He wasn't exactly sure why he'd even lied in the *first* place. Maybe it was as simple as the fact that he'd much rather be Drew Van Allen, college student, home from Princeton for a family emergency than Drew Van Allen, high school junior with two completely screwed-up parents and an avalanche of confusion stampeding through his brain on an hourly basis. It wasn't like he couldn't man up and tell her the truth at any time, but somehow, now that the lie was out there, he felt powerless to dispel it.

Olivia leaned forward reflexively, her center of gravity off, then collapsed onto the ice, her ass hitting the cold, wet surface with a smack. "Owww!" she whined, looking up at Drew and giggling, reaching one hand underneath her to rub the back of her jeans-covered legs where they'd made contact with the ice. "That really hurt!" she said mournfully as Drew pulled her up, watching as she brushed the back of her jeans off with her red-mittened hands. So far anyway, college girls didn't seem all that different from the high school girls he was used to. The only differences he had noted thus far were that college girls wore less makeup—and definitely seemed to complain less, too. They'd been on the ice for a better part of an hour, and not once had Olivia pointed out how cold it was outside, or made him stop every ten minutes so that she could check her reflection in her compact and apply more lip gloss—a move that basically defined the lip liner–wielding presence of one Madison Macallister.

Drew felt a sharp pain in his chest as he thought about Madison and Casey, and the way things had gone down. He'd wanted so badly to pull Casey aside this afternoon on the steps and apologize, to tell her that it wasn't her, that it was *him*, that he was so screwed up that lately all he seemed capable of doing was making a mess of things—including their relationship—or whatever it was that had been happening between them. But she was sitting there with Darin, who was a pretty good guy, a guy, Drew knew, who would treat her right, who would never even consider walking out of a party and leaving her standing there alone. And, if, by some bizarre twist of fate, Darin did happen to hurt her, Drew was almost certain he would've called her the next morning to apologize. Hell, Darin Hollingsworth probably would show up at her doorstep with a bouquet of roses. And Drew knew that as much as he hated the idea of it, as much as it hurt his chest to look at her every day and not talk to her, that Casey, as special as she was, deserved a guy like Darin—not someone who was so messed up that he kept hurting anyone who was unfortunate enough to get close to him . . . Somehow, with Olivia it was easier, simply because it wasn't *real*.

"So," Drew said once she righted herself and they began gliding across the ice again, this time side by side, hands entwined, except with those damn mittens she was wearing it felt like holding hands with a stuffed toy instead of a hot girl, which Olivia definitely was. "What's your major?"

Olivia took a deep breath in and exhaled, sending a cloud of breath into the night air. "English," she said decisively. "I mean, it's my mother tongue—I figure I can't screw it up *too* badly, you know?" She laughed, pulling a strand of hair from the corner of her mouth with her free hand. "What are you studying at Princeton?"

Drew felt his heart accelerate and a cold sweat begin to break out on his palms. Good thing she was wearing those mittens after all . . . "I'm not sure," he said nervously. "I'm just . . . taking a lot of different classes, trying to figure out where my interests lie, you know?" Drew panicked a bit in the subsequent silence. Did he sound too high school? Too unfocused? Or basically just like every other majorless moron Olivia had met at college so far? After a moment, Olivia nodded, and Drew exhaled heavily, relieved that he seemed to have said the right thing. "I'm really into film though."

"Oh yeah? Who's your favorite director?" Olivia asked, further confirming Drew's newfound opinion of the awesomeness of college girls. Casey had talked to him about movies, sure, but coming from Olivia it seemed like there was no doubt that he was a film buff, that those were the type of people she was around all of the time. That was the kind of girl that Drew wanted, those were the kind of people he wanted to be around.

"Woody Allen," Drew said, hoping that his answer would be cool enough, that she didn't think he was a romantic or passé or stupid for not saying Godard or Bresson.

"La di da, la la," Olivia replied, doing her best to do Diane Keaton's little head nod thing while balancing precariously on two very narrow blades of steel. "*Annie Hall* is probably my favorite film of all time. Can't say that I'm not a real New Yorker now, can you?" Olivia teased, glancing at him sideways under her lashes, which Drew noticed were preternaturally long and thick.

That was it. Drew was in. This thing with Olivia—whatever it was—was something new and different and totally effortless and, above all, *fun*. It felt like there was no pretense with Olivia, no rules. *And she loved Woody Allen.* Part of him considered proposing for that fact alone. *I wonder how she feels about Almodóvar,* he wondered distractedly. Before he knew it, he was speaking again, not really realizing the exact consequences of what he was asking, but even as his mind caught up with his mouth, he found himself not caring—this was too good to have a lie get in the way.

"So there's this thing going on next week. It's like a holiday party. A gala." He paused, not wanting to seem too excited, trying to maintain a slight bit of nonchalance.

"And?" Olivia asked, her eyebrows raised, an adorable grin spread across her face.

"And, well, I was hoping that you might go with me." Drew exhaled and gave Olivia a tentative, sideways grin, feeling his heart begin to race wildly, his pulse throbbing in his temples. Why was asking girls out so stressful? Every time he did it, Drew felt like he was having a stroke. "It's not the Chrysler Building, but I think you'd find it acceptable for a second date . . . or whatever you want to call it."

Olivia smiled, and the ice surrounding Drew's vital organs melted a little more as he gazed at her heart-shaped face, which looked as smooth as vanilla ice cream and twice as sweet, her incredibly blue eyes that bordered on violet. "Just acceptable, huh?" she said jokingly. "What kind of dive is this thing at?"

"Uh, the Guggenheim," Drew deadpanned.

After a moment's silence that was rapidly filled with a truly horrific version of "God Rest Ye Merry Gentlemen" blaring from the speakers, Olivia burst out laughing, squeezing his hand just a little tighter with her own in the process.

"The Guggenheim?" She giggled, feigning wide-eyed naïveté. "As in the large circular building? The museum with no corners? You're inviting me to the Holiday Gala at the Guggenheim?"

Drew blushed, trying to wipe his suddenly running nose nonchalantly with his free hand before it got totally out of control. "Well . . . *yeah*," he said, hoping to God she didn't say no, despite the disastrous consequences that might befall him for asking her there.

"I don't know, Drew . . ." Olivia said teasingly, a singsong note in her voice as her speech trailed off into the air, leaving him hanging. "Oh my *God*," she exclaimed, letting go of his hand to playfully shove him in the upper arm. "Of *course* I'll go with you!" she finished, her dark eyes alive with excitement. "I'd love to. But you're not off the hook on the Chrysler thing . . . that'll just have to be pushed back to date number three."

Drew smiled nervously, and let go of her hand, using it as an excuse to push his hair back. How did they get to date number three all of a sudden? Did he even *want* a third date—along with the subsequent pressure? Wasn't having a third date just a hop, skip, and a jump from having an actual *relationship*?

As he skated along, trying to figure it all out, a little boy in a bright red jacket and hockey skates whizzed by, knocking into Olivia with his Tonka-truck-wide body with a loud smacking sound. Drew watched as she wobbled precariously on her blades, reaching out his arms to catch her at the last moment before her ass became one with the ice yet again. As she pitched forward in his arms, leaning heavily against his chest in a soft bundle of cashmere that smelled like the fresh, clean snow that hadn't yet fallen, mixed with some perfume that reminded him, insanely enough, of hot chocolate, Drew couldn't deny that, third date or not, he was extremely attracted to this girl.

Olivia raised her head, her violet eyes searching his own without words as she leaned in and, with a smile, pressed her lips to his. Drew closed his eyes, leaning into the kiss, his arms reaching out to wrap themselves around her body, pulling her even closer. Even though he was doing a pretty good impersonation of someone lost in the throes of passion, Drew couldn't keep his mind from running nonstop, even with Olivia's warm breath on his face, her soft lips that opened and closed as she kissed him more deeply. *Can I really make this work*, Drew wondered as she pulled away, her deeply blue-violet eyes glimmering in the glow from the huge tree hanging above them, *when the whole relationship is pretty much based on lies?*

"Is there something wrong?" Olivia asked nervously, biting her bottom lip as she took in Drew's obvious confusion.

"Nothing at all," Drew said reassuringly as he pulled her close once again, leaning in for another kiss, determined not to worry anymore. *Lies, truth—it's all pretty relative, right? Be-*

192

sides, it's only a little white lie anyway—the kind that won't hurt anybody, Drew told himself as he dissolved into their kiss once again, tangling his hands in Olivia's mass of dark, silky hair. After all, stretching the truth had definitely worked for his parents for all these years. Why should he be any different?

uptown lounge

"Don't you want to sit a little closer to me?"

Jared smiled, parting his full lips, a playful expression enlivening his face, his dark hair falling forward and obscuring his blue eyes momentarily before he pushed it back with one hand, his expression turning confident as he reached across the table, encircling Phoebe's wrist gently in his huge hand and pulling softly until she had no choice but to lean across the wooden surface and kiss him, her lips melting into his, the room alive with arcs of golden light dancing behind her closed eyelids. Jared's other hand rested lightly in the hair that fell down her back like dark water, stroking it lightly. The touch of his fingers on her scalp made Phoebe want to curl up in his arms and purr like a contented kitty. But as attracted as she was to Jared physically, every time she closed her eyes, Drew's face inevitably rose up from the darkness and implanted itself on her brain, twisting her thoughts like rigatoni, and throwing her heart into traitorous, unchecked mutiny.

After an hour and a half of trading stories about their screwed-up parents, and drinking enough coffee to give a small child caffeine-induced seizures, Drew and Phoebe had stood awkwardly on the sidewalk outside Uncommon Grounds, Phoebe scuffing the toe of her ballet flats obsessively against the pavement, afraid that if she kept standing there for even one more moment she'd become paralyzed by the intensity and uncertainty in Drew's sleep-deprived, anguished blue eyes. Whatever connection they shared, Phoebe couldn't help but think it might be more than just physical—way more. Or maybe she was just reading too much into the fact that their parents were currently sharing more than just decorating tips . . . Phoebe frowned, her lips leaving Jared's in a burst of confusion with a soft smack.

Phoebe stared into Jared's eyes, watching as they slowly and unabashedly traveled their way down her body from her smooth, pale face to the black Azzedine Alaia dress that hugged her body like an extremely chic wetsuit. *Was this all they really had?* Phoebe wondered nervously, sitting back against the purple banquette and willing Jared to look up and hold her gaze at eye level, to ask how her day was, how she was holding up—anything but continue the obvious game of Guess the Cup Size he was currently engrossed in. Sure, everything was great now—when everything was all brand-spanking-new—but

Phoebe couldn't help wondering what might happen if and when they got sick of making out with one another, when things weren't so new anymore . . . or forbidden.

They may have been making out in a dark lounge, but since Sophie had given them her blessing, hiding was hardly a necessity. A cold wave moved up and down Phoebe's body, the opposite of the heat wave that usually sent her thighs up in flames whenever Jared was anywhere in the immediate vicinity. Until now, her relationship with Jared was the only stable thing she had in her life—the only part of her messed-up existence that actually seemed to be working out, and now *that* was completely shot to shit . . .

Madonna's *Hard Candy* blared from the speakers, drowning out the hope of having any sort of conversation that required actual listening, the room filling with the Material Girl's nasal, slightly imperious vocal stylings. *Can't get my head around it, I need to think about it* . . .

Story of my life, Phoebe thought with a weak smile, sitting back in her chair and looking around at the fashionable crowd of Upper East Siders who were populating The Lounge, touching their full martini glasses together, the musical clinking mixing with the staccato click of Jimmy Choos traipsing across the hardwood floors and the high-pitched, sucking noise of vigorous air-kissing.

Make that ass-kissing, Phoebe thought with a scowl, resting her elbows on the wooden table and playing with the red plastic stirrer in her vodka martini, pulling it out to pop a salty green olive between her teeth. When she'd agreed to meet

Jared for drinks, she'd hoped that this would turn out to be the kind of night where they could find somewhere quiet to sit around and just *talk*. But The Lounge, with its dark corners and romantic lighting, long cherrywood bar, jewel-toned color scheme in shades of crimson and glossy metallic purple, and small plates of hip bar food that were meant for sharing, was seemingly designed to get couples to do anything *but* talk.

"Want to come over tonight?" Jared asked with a grin, just as their server dropped a plate of Pan Asian vegetable dumplings with plum sauce in the center of the table, the fragrant steam rising from the white porcelain like secrets being dispersed into the air. Jared snapped his chopsticks in half, rubbing the two sticks against one another to remove any stray splinters of wood, then attacked the plate, chewing rapidly. Phoebe prodded the plump skin of the dumpling with one chopstick, then placed it down on the table again and took a swallow of vodka instead.

"Why?" Phoebe answered absentmindedly, the words spilling from her lips before she could check herself. She smiled to cover up the hastiness of her reply, and popped another olive into her mouth.

"Why do you think?" Jared smiled naughtily, raising one eyebrow in that maddening way of his that usually made Phoebe want to rip off his shirt and blindfold him with the scraps of fabric so that he could never, ever get away from her. But now, when all she wanted to do was connect with him on *any* other level but physical, it was just annoying.

"I wish," Phoebe said quickly. "I have a lot of homework I

have to finish before tomorrow." Her cheeks flushed beneath her Nars Orgasm blush that flecked her pale skin with tiny gold particles. God, she hated lying—it always made her feel so dirty and compromised, not to mention an exact clone of her cheating, lying, scheming society robot of a mother.

"That's cool," Jared said, spearing another dumpling and popping it in his mouth. "What about the gala on Friday? You're going with me to that, right?" Jared swallowed, wiped his hand on a purple linen napkin, and balled it up, tossing it onto the table, his actions betraying what his voice did not— that he was slightly irritated.

Phoebe twirled a strand of dark hair around one finger, as she tried to think of what to say. She was Jared's girlfriend, right? Then of course she *had* to go with him to the biggest social event on the winter party circuit. Phoebe frowned, playing with the stirrer in her drink. Shouldn't she want to go with him—and what did it mean that she suddenly kind of *didn't*? That she couldn't seem to stop herself from wondering if Drew was going, and, if so, who, exactly, he'd be bringing with him. *It's just a crush*, she told herself. *It's like a fever— you'll feel lousy for a few days, but then it will break.* It *had* to. But what if it didn't? And why was she suddenly so afraid?

"Yeah—of course!" Phoebe answered, looking up with a brilliant smile that felt about as fake to her as the rows of Louis Vuitton handbags littering Canal Street—otherwise known as fake bag nirvana for the bridge-and-tunnel set. *Act normal,* she told herself steadily as Jared reached across the table again and pressed his mouth to hers, the sweet-and-salty plum sauce mingling with the taste of his lips. *Act normal and soon maybe it won't be just an act*, Phoebe silently reassured herself as she opened her mouth and kissed him back, determined now to get things between her and Jared back on track, and her heart back where it belonged.

british invasion

Casey leaned against the door of her grandmother's apartment at The Bram, grateful to be home. The day had dragged on forever, and there had been no hope at all of concentrating in her afternoon classes at all after Drew's little visit on the steps. Plus, as she was walking home, Darin had called to invite her to some fancy-pants party at the Guggenheim on Friday night, and, as usual, she had less than nothing to wear. On top of everything else, Meadowlark had suddenly turned into college central with everyone freaking out about the impending SATs—lunch hours were now routinely filled with practice sessions, tables littered with calculators and study guides instead of nail polish and the current issue of *InStyle*.

Casey didn't know what was worse—having to balance her

tuna salad on a Pearson's book, or the fear that had begun to overtake her about the SATs in general. She'd never exactly been what you might call a natural-born test-taker—usually her palms got all sweaty and then she would promptly forget everything she'd spent the last two weeks trying to cram into her brain. And unlike the majority of Meadlowlark, Casey had two choices—get a scholarship or attend Illinois State back in Normal where her mother taught Women's Studies, as children of tenured faculty members had the added bonus of free tuition. But the last thing she wanted now was to go back home—her life there now seemed like something that had happened to someone else entirely, like a movie she'd slept through without even knowing it. Which, of course, brought her back to the obvious problem of having nothing to wear to the gala . . .

Casey pulled her phone from her overstuffed black tote, and began to text Phoebe, her fingers moving quickly over the keypad. Even though Pulse had given her an ample amount of clothes, none of them constituted anything she could even think about wearing to a museum gala.

Darin asked me to the gala!—but no dress! Can u help?

Casey waited for the screen to begin to flash with Phoebe's response, which it did almost immediately as Phoebe was, hands down, the fastest texter among The Bram Clan. *Her phone should just be stapled to her hand,* Casey thought, smiling. *It would make her life so much easier . . .*

Have just the thing. You like blue, right?

Casey nodded at the screen as if Phoebe could actually see her response. Blue, green, chartreuse—whatever. If she was borrowing it, she wasn't exactly going to be picky about it . . .

"Casey Anne McCloy, is that you?"

Casey's gray eyes widened in shock as her mother, Barbara McCloy, came striding into the hall wearing a long blue-and-yellow batik-printed skirt with a pair of navy thermal leggings underneath, and a yellow sweater that had clearly seen better days as the wool was unraveling at the bottom, dangling like strands of tangled hair. And speaking of hair, Barbara's yellow mane, the exact shade and hue as her daughter's, was scraped back in her signature bun, the strands pulled so tight that Casey was always afraid her mother's eyes would someday be catapulted from their sockets only to bounce around the room like slightly squishy Ping-Pong balls. A pair of rectangular navy eyeglasses that Casey had never seen before sat on the bridge of her nose, magnifying her eyes, which were speckled and flecked like a blue-gray pebble.

"So, my prodigal daughter is finally home from the wars," Barbara said with a tight smile, her voice clipped and annoyingly Anglofied as she walked over and enfolded her daughter in a hug. Casey's senses were suddenly enveloped in the series of scents that always brought Barbara to mind: lavender talcum powder, spilled ink, and the musty, dusty tang of old libraries mixed with the intoxicating, comforting smell of ancient, leather-bound books. Barbara let go, holding her at arm's length as her eyes traveled the length of Casey's body, missing nothing, taking in her dark denim jeans and plaid trench, the pair of chrome Chanel shades Phoebe had given her, which neatly held back her mass of straightened hair. Her mother's lips turned up in a half-smile before she spoke, her voice ringing out loudly in the foyer as she reached over and picked up a piece of Casey's hair, holding it for a moment between her fingers, then dropping it like it was a dead bird. "And by wars, clearly I'm referring to the consuming frenzy, into which you have so *obviously* been recruited."

"It's just straightened," Casey said nervously, snapping her cell phone shut and tossing it back into her bag, trying to blow off her mother's fixation on all things fashionable—which meant, in Barbara-speak, all things evilly commercial. "And these sunglasses aren't even *mine*," she said, snatching them off the top of her head and holding them out for Barbara to inspect. "I'm just borrowing them," she added as if that would make any real difference to her mother, who thought that Target was upscale, and that paying any more than thirty dollars for a pair of shoes meant that you should be promptly folded into a straitjacket and carried off to the nearest padded cell—pronto. "I thought you weren't coming back until next week," Casey said, her voice registering her surprise, but not, she hoped, her horror.

"I see we have a lot to talk about," Barbara said dryly, putting an arm around Casey and leading her into Nanna's cheery blue-and-white living room with its sheer white curtains and powder blue furniture—a space that always seemed vaguely nautical, and made her feel more like she was on a boat heading out to sea rather than sitting on a puffy, pale blue sofa in one of the most exclusive apartment buildings on the Upper East Side.

"How was school today?" Nanna shouted out from her armchair, her white hair the exact color of the pearls looped around her neck, shining in the rapidly receding daylight. "Break any hearts?" Nanna added, cackling softly to herself before pausing to sigh exasperatedly over the ball of yellow wool in her lap, holding up one of her silver knitting needles and pointing it at Casey in a way that seemed vaguely menacing—well, as menacing as a little old lady in a pewter gray twin set could possibly be. "Whatever made me think I needed to take up this nonsense in the first place?" Nanna muttered, dropping the needle to her lap and throwing the ball of tangled wool onto the floor, then kicking at the yellow mess with one of the many pairs of vintage black Chanel ballet flats she was fond of wearing. Nanna was forever taking up appropriately grandmotherish hobbies like baking and knitting, but strictly for show. When no one was looking, Casey knew that she often threw the tangled wool or the mess of horrifyingly burnt-to-a-crisp cookies right in the trash.

"So, why are you back early?" Casey asked again, ignoring Nanna completely. "I mean," she went on hurriedly, sitting down and promptly sinking into the bowl of pale blue whipped cream that masqueraded as a sofa, "I'm glad to see you, but you had said you were coming back on the twentieth."

"I had a change of plans," Barbara said with a sigh as she

plopped down next to Casey on the sofa, her newfound British accent making her sound like she should've been granting an audience to the Queen instead of a lowly commoner like her own daughter. "And I wanted to find out just what in God's name you've gotten yourself into with this *ridiculous* TV program." Barbara rolled her eyes, clearly both annoyed and wanting an explanation. Now.

"Well, I think I'll take this opportunity to enjoy Alex Trebek in the privacy of my own bedroom." Nanna grinned, standing up and kicking the wool out of the way with the toe of her slipper.

"Not so fast," Barbara snapped, pointing her finger at Nanna—a move that stopped the diminutive white-haired woman in her tracks. "Care to explain exactly *why* you thought it was a good idea to allow Casey to do this without consulting me?"

"I *did* consult you." Nanna blinked, her face expressionless. Casey recognized that look. It was the same expression Nanna wore every time she cheated at one of her bridge games.

Barbara laughed, her expression incredulous. "Mom, you called me *after* you'd signed the papers, just to let me know!" Barbara threw up her hands in exasperation before crossing them sulkily over her chest.

"Details, details," Nanna cackled with a wave of her hand, then promptly turned on her heel and walked out of the room before Barbara could say anything else.

"I mean, you can't be serious about this thing, can you,

Casey? Shows like this are just hugely problematic on so, so many levels. Just look at the way you're dressing already—it's like watching a product placement circus," Barbara said, her voice rising to a pitch that anyone who was born speaking with her new accent would consider to be extremely uncouth. "And let's not even get started on the way they portray women! Do you really want to be one of those girls?"

Casey bounced up from the sofa and began pacing back and forth in front of the long windows that looked out across the park. It was totally the moment she had been dreading—and it wasn't just the fact that Barbara was mad at her. It was the way that she—her daughter, her own flesh and blood—had been immediately turned into some kind of case study that was being subjected to the most scrutinizing academic analysis. She had been doing this as long as Casey could remember, starting on the night when her mother found her underneath the covers playing with a contraband Barbie by flashlight. Not that the young Casey had any idea what the Dominant Narrative was or what exactly bell hooks had said in that one essay, but she had hated being treated like the subject of a research paper then, and she definitely hated it now.

Casey stared at her mother, unable to deny how closely they resembled one another—the same yellow hair, the same gray eyes, the same stubborn demeanor. She knew from past experiences that it was important to remain calm, no matter how desperate and out of control she felt. It was bizarre—the minute Casey got around her mother, she found herself barely able to stop from acting out, from trying to define herself against the woman who'd raised her, to make it clear that they were nothing at all alike.

"Don't do this, Mom," she said slowly, levelly, holding her mother's gray eyes with her own. "This isn't your classroom; it's my life. I want to do this and I *like* the way that it's changed me. I'm not that sweaty mess of curly hair that was shipped out here from Illinois at the beginning of the year." Casey stopped pacing and stood straight in front of her mother who still sat on the couch, looking strangely relaxed, probably due to the fact that she had sat through many a Casey McCloy summing-it-all-up monologue in the past. "I'm actually starting to fit *in*, which I even had a hard time doing in *Normal* of all places." With that, Casey flopped back down next to her mother, exhausted from all of the emotions that had been welling up and getting all over everything, making an absolute mess of what had been an already emotionally messy day.

"I'm glad to hear that you're fitting in," Barbara said after a momentary silence punctuated only by screams from *Jeopardy!*—which was playing at a volume in the next room that could only be described as deafening. Barbara was beginning to sound more like a mother and less like a professor, the lines in her brow softening as she went on. "This isn't the easiest place to do that," she said, waving her hands around, pointing out the window. "But you just have to remember— and I'm saying this as your *mother*—to keep a hold of yourself, Casey Anne McCloy. And I *know* that you can do that."

"Blah, blah, blah," Casey joked and she reached over to hug her mom, finally, truly glad to see her now that the confrontation was dying down. "And don't worry, Mom. You don't have to take any part in the whole thing—there's no way I'm letting you anywhere near the cameras. The last thing I need is one of your diatribes ending up on national television." Casey shuddered, the very thought making her feel almost queasy.

"I'll just keep my diatribe to the paper I'm going to write—and don't even think that you can stop me," Barbara said smugly, pushing her glasses farther up on the bridge of her nose. "I can see it now, published in *The Oxford Review* or *Critical Inquiry—Stepford Child: The Social Engineering of America's Newest Reality TV Star.*"

Casey blinked uncomprehendingly, her gray eyes struggling not to reveal the sense of absolute horror she was currently experiencing. That was literally the worst idea she'd ever heard, not to mention the most potentially embarrassing. "You have your dreams and I have mine," Casey said weakly, curling her head into the space between her mother's jawline and collarbone, just like she had when she was a baby. "But you're going to have to come up with a new title—that one's probably going to be longer than the article."

"True," Barbara said sleepily, her jet lag definitely starting to kick in as she closed her eyes and began to breathe evenly. Speaking of dreams, Casey wondered if she was even right: Did she have any left? If so, she wasn't exactly sure what they were these days. At first all she'd wanted was to fit in with Madison and The Bram Clan, and that longing was like a constant weight in her heart that she seemed to carry around with her all the time, like a manhole cover strapped to her chest. Then, all she'd wanted was Drew—to finally have a boyfriend who was more than just a passing crush—and it was obvious how *that* had turned out. And now she wasn't sure if it was safe to believe in dreams at all anymore. Maybe at the end of the day, believing that you really could get what you wanted was just too idealistic a notion in the relentless, dog-eat-dog world of the big city—or maybe she really *was* beginning to fit in to the Upper East Side scene . . . in ways she'd never even considered . . . and with consequences that made her almost glad that her mother, as annoying as she could definitely be most of the time, was suddenly back in town.

silver bells

Drew squirmed in the confines of his black Armani suit crossed with fine gray pinstripes, and tugged resentfully at the collar of his white dress shirt, surreptitiously smoothing the black-and-violet-flecked tie that was knotted around his neck like a noose. He hated wearing a suit—he always felt like he was being strangled, and the added torture of a tie only served to amplify the sensation that he was merely a few shallow breaths away from having his respiration cut off altogether. As uncomfortable as he felt all decked out like a prize pony, it couldn't begin to detract from the happiness he felt looking around the interior of the Guggenheim, his favorite museum in all of Manhattan. His blue eyes happily swept over the brilliant white walls that curved around and around in the circular building, as he craned his neck upward to take in the aerial view of the upper floors that circled around like the outside of a beehive.

The Guggenheim, a refuge for some of the greatest modern art on the entire planet, had gone all-out this year. An enormous avant-garde ice sculpture loomed over the front of the room on a long, red metallic table, the frozen liquid crafted into the shape of a spiky winter tree sans leaves, its icy transparent branches reaching hopefully toward the sky. Huge aluminum Christmas trees were scattered around the room, their shiny silver branches aglow with tiny white lights. Clusters of tables were strategically placed throughout the enormous space, covered with silver tablecloths that sparkled in the whiteness of the building itself that seemed to encroach on everything in the immediate vicinity. Miniature solid steel cubes filled with white candles illuminated the centerpieces of pine garlands, silver acorns, and holly, red berries peeking out festively from the dark green leaves.

"So, how do you like NYU?" Drew asked, leaning a bit closer, and breathing in the scent of her perfume, which smelled almost exactly like the sweet scent of Coppertone mixed with a field of wildflowers—floral, weirdly almost salty, and yet comfortingly familiar.

"It's okay, I guess," Olivia said after a pause. She reached over with her long fingers and toyed with the crystal stem of the almost-empty champagne flute that rested on the table in front of her. "It's harder than I thought it would be," she added thoughtfully, flashing him a grin that seemed almost apologetic.

"In what way?" Drew asked, genuinely curious, not to mention relieved that the topic of conversation was, for once, not himself. Sitting there talking to Olivia felt so natural, like they'd known each other for years instead of just a few short days.

"Well, most of my friends ended up going to school out of state," Olivia began with a sigh. "But, I don't know . . . I grew up on the Upper West Side, and I just really never wanted to live anywhere else, you know?"

Drew nodded eagerly in agreement, mentally ticking off the plusses in Olivia's favor: smart, beautiful, likes Woody Allen, *and* admits of her own free will that New York is really the only city worth living in! What more could he possibly want? But as Drew looked at her, noticing her absurdly full, bow-shaped upper lip as she picked up her glass and drained the remaining dregs of pale, golden liquid, Drew had to admit to himself that his attraction to Olivia also had something to do with the fact that she had absolutely nothing to do with Meadowlark, his social circle, or his life up until now.

"So, in a weird way, I guess I've had to start all over again," Olivia said quietly, running her hand over the tablecloth, smoothing the material against her palm. "Which is totally bizarre, considering I grew up here!" She laughed, running a hand through her hair self-consciously, her cheeks and throat flushing in the wake of her sudden confession. "If you want the truth," she said soberly, serious now, her violet eyes meeting his and holding them steadily, "I guess I've just been a little lonely lately."

Drew looked at the way Olivia's dark hair fell around her heart-shaped face in soft waves, at the naked pain in her violet eyes, and felt a surge of connection between them. "I know what that's like," Drew answered after a long moment. "I mean, lately I've been feeling like I need to start all over again, too—and it's been kind of hard." Drew swallowed and looked away, mentally willing himself not to get emotional.

"Maybe . . ." Olivia said after a pause, looking down at her hands, "we could start over together?" The last word came out as a question, the inflection in her voice rising high and unsure at the end of the sentence.

"Do you want some more champagne?" Drew asked, leaning toward Olivia so that she could hear him above the string quartet decked out in tuxedos, who were planted firmly in the far corner of the room and had just then begun to play. He placed his hand gently atop her thigh, the warmth from her leg seeping into his hand, giving him a flesh-induced contact high that was suddenly bordering on severe.

"Always," Olivia said, smiling warmly, her violet eyes sparkling mischievously, her dark hair hanging in soft waves that rippled down her back and over the soft fabric of the free-flowing ivory gown she wore. Drew didn't know what these types of dresses were called, exactly—all he *did* know was that the perfectly draped silky material looked like it had been ripped off a Greek statue at the Met and tailored to fit Olivia's body specifically.

Drew got up, pushing in his chair and heading over to the bar at the far end of the room, his mind racing with possibilities.

He knew now, as if there had ever really been a doubt in his mind, that if he really wanted to keep things going with this girl he was going to have to tell her he had lied to her—not to mention the truth about the fact that he was still in high school. He'd invited her to the Holiday Gala, for God's sake! Considering the fact that his entire school would most likely be in attendance, it was a move that not only bordered on stupid, it was positively *suicidal*.

"Hey, Drew," a tentative voice said at his back. Drew turned around to see Casey standing there, her yellow silky hair falling onto her shoulders, the sprinkling of freckles across the bridge of her nose that he'd always loved clearly visible on her translucent skin, a cobalt blue dress made of some satiny material that reminded him, bizarrely, of wrapping paper draped across her body, falling to her knees. Drew noticed that she was blushing furiously, her face rapidly turning a shade of red that looked almost painful.

"Hey," he said, with a nervous smile. "Good to see you." Drew leaned forward and kissed her on the cheek, resting his hands lightly on her bare shoulders, wondering if at any moment she was going to reach out and slap him—not that he'd really blame her if she actually did. "You're here with Darin?" he asked, scanning the crowd for Hollingsworth's skinny frame.

"Yeah," Casey answered, almost apologetically, blushing harder. "I'm just grabbing us some drinks."

"Me, too," Drew said, gesturing toward the bar with one hand, a tiny spark of jealousy detonating in his chest, which he promptly attempted to squash with irrefutable logic. *Hollingsworth's a good guy*, he told himself, hoping if he said it enough, he'd stop wanting to rip his head from his shoulders every time he saw them together. *Besides, you had your shot with her and you blew it. As usual.* There was an awkward silence as they looked at one another, millions of unasked and unanswered questions floating around in Casey's gray eyes.

"You're here with . . ." Casey asked, gesturing with her hand to Olivia—who was still back at the table—her voice trailing off into silence.

"I just met her a few days ago," Drew said offhandedly, not really wanting to get into it. "I tried to call you the other night," he said, changing the subject and taking a deep breath.

"I know," Casey said quietly, biting her bottom lip. "But I . . ."

"It's cool," Drew interrupted, cutting her off before she could finish. "I mean, I probably wouldn't talk to me either if I were you."

"It's not that," Casey said, her brow creased with confusion. "I just don't understand . . . what happened. I mean, you just ran *out* that night at Sophie's party, and I really haven't heard from you *since*."

"I know," Drew said with a sigh, knowing that if he didn't apologize to her right then, in person, he just wasn't going to be able to live with it. "Things at home have been pretty rough, and I've been acting like an asshole. I'm really, really sorry I left that night, and I'm even sorrier that I screwed up things with us so badly."

Casey smiled faintly, her gray eyes suddenly misty with emotion. "Thanks," she said quietly, looking away. "I really needed to hear that." Drew looked down at his own empty hands, unsure what to say or do next. "Anyway," Casey went on, clearing her throat while looking back at Drew and smiling. "I should probably get back."

"Me, too," Drew said, relieved that he'd finally apologized. It felt like a two-thousand-ton boulder had just been removed from his back. "I'll see you later."

"Later," Casey answered, turning around to walk away, and stopping to glance back at him over her shoulder, her gray eyes still filled with questions Drew knew he wasn't capable of answering right now—as much as he might've liked to.

As he stood there, watching her walk away from him and toward another guy, he realized that maybe lying had worked for his parents all these years, but Drew now knew that he couldn't agree to that kind of don't-ask-don't-tell policy in his own romantic relationships. He'd already pretty much destroyed his chances with both Mad and Casey, and he was damned if the same thing was going to happen with Olivia. He wanted to get to *know* her—without lies and deceit getting in the way and forcing a wedge between them the way it had with his own parents. Most of all, he didn't want to be that guy—the guy who lied just so he could hook up with some random girl, who didn't even question whether or not sleeping around constituted a kind of betrayal. Regardless of how his parents couched it, or whatever bizarre rules they'd put into place in order to hold the torn fabric of their marriage together, Drew knew that it was *history*. And the only thing he was sure of right now was that he didn't want to be that guy—ever again.

Drew took two gently frothing champagne flutes from a tuxedoed, slightly disheveled hipster bartender, a pair of tortoiseshell glasses perched on the bridge of his nose, his brown slightly spiky hair shining in the overhead lighting, and downed one glass quickly before grabbing a replacement.

"How's the champagne?" the bartender inquired in a friendly monotone.

"It's great," Drew answered immediately, without even stopping to wonder why he was being asked such a completely inane question.

"You hated it," the bartender deadpanned, a slight smile tilting his lips up at one corner.

"No, it was fine," Drew said, bemused by the whole encounter, which was getting more surreal by the moment.

"You totally hated it," the bartender answered without hesitation, chuckling to himself as he began filling empty champagne flutes with the frothy, golden liquid.

Drew shook his head from side to side as he walked away, amazed by the complete randomness of Manhattan, how even the bartenders were constantly auditioning for God knew what. He slowly began pushing through the crowd and back to the table, trying to work up his courage. *Just man up and explain*, he thought, trying to convince himself, but his words, no matter how forcefully he repeated them, felt hollow and flimsy—even from the protected confines of his own head. *If she really likes you, she'll understand.* But would she? Or would she just get mad and stomp off in a huff? Lately, it seemed like way too much of that kind of stuff had been happening in his world, and he was, all at once, so very tired of it. Drew walked determinedly back toward the table, bracing himself for what he now knew he had to do, his heart racing crazily. As he handed the glass to Olivia, she looked up at him and smiled, just as the quartet broke into a strings-only version of "White Christmas."

"Wanna dance?" she asked, raising an eyebrow coquettishly.

Drew smiled, tilting his head back and draining his glass in one prolonged swallow, and thumped it back on the table. "Hell yeah," he said, reaching out and taking her small, soft hand in his, and leading her to the packed dance floor, where he was immediately enveloped in clouds of heavy, opulent perfumes that smelled like the incense that had drifted through the halls of the cold, stone churches he'd visited in Rome last summer on a weekend trip—sweet, rich, and slightly spicy, like the scent of skin itself.

Drew leaned into Olivia's slim frame as she wound her arms around his neck, looking deeply into his eyes. He found himself mesmerized by their violet depths, unable to look away. If he was going to tell her, he was going to have to do it now.

"So . . ." Drew said carefully, feeling suddenly vulnerable, and unable to meet her eyes. Instead, he concentrated his gaze over her shoulder and at the front entrance. "There's something I really need to tell you."

"You're married?" Olivia deadpanned, her rose-colored lips turning up in a small smile.

"God forbid," Drew scoffed, taking a deep breath and meeting her gaze before he completely lost what was left of his courage. *Suck it up*, he told himself, *and just tell her. If she runs, then she runs, and you'll pick up the pieces and move on, the same way you always do . . .* Except it wouldn't be the same, would it? Because he'd know that he'd hurt her, that he'd blown a chance at something special—for the third time in less than two months.

"So what is it?" Olivia asked, crinkling her brow and staring at him with an expression that was equal parts expectation and trepidation, the fear clearly winning out at the end, clouding her lovely violet eyes and making the hairs on Drew's arms stand up on end. "You can tell me," Olivia said gently, "whatever it is, I'm sure I'll understand."

Drew looked at her expectant face, her long, white arms wrapped around his neck, her sweet, floral perfume filling his senses, and knew right then and there that he just couldn't do it, that the words, no matter how badly he wanted them to come out, just weren't ready. Out of the corner of his eyes, Drew watched as Madison and Sophie walked through the front entrance, Madison's gaze scanning the dance floor and coming to rest on Drew and Olivia, her green eyes narrowing murderously.

"Olivia, I really like you," Drew said weakly, dropping his gaze to the floor, red-faced and completely frustrated with himself. When exactly had he become such a spineless liar? If this wasn't the person he wanted to be then why did he feel so powerless to change things? If he didn't tell her now, he knew Madison would take great and calculated pleasure in doing so. But somehow, the threat of this wasn't quite enough to get him to open his mouth and speak. He just wanted one perfect moment, one moment that wasn't ruined completely. All he really wanted was to dance with this girl, uninterrupted. Then maybe he could figure out what to do next.

Olivia giggled softly with pleasure and surprise, leaning a little closer and tightening her hold around his neck. "I like you, too," she answered back as she touched her lips to his. The moment her mouth began to open under his, the room, the terrible Christmas music, the feeling that had followed Drew everywhere lately—a combination of despair and a shaking nervousness—began to slowly ebb away, the panic and uncertainty of the last month evaporating in the heat of her kiss.

what comes around goes around

⊖

Madison Macallister stepped into the shockingly white room, Sophie trailing behind her like an apparition in a Stella McCartney gold, knee-length cocktail dress, her honey-colored hair twisted into a seashell whorl at the back of her neck. Madison looked down appreciatively at her own red satin Gucci halter dress that tied around the neck, exposing a deep but tasteful keyhole of flesh, and that flared out festively around her knees. Her newly painted, cherry-red pedicure sparkled from the confines of her gold Dior sandals encrusted with rows of red Swarovski crystals. Madison looked around the crowded room, taking in the aluminum trees, the enormous ice sculpture looming over the front of the room, her green eyes squinting slightly in the glare. The Guggenheim was so . . . *white*. You practically had to wear sunglasses just to deal with the goddamn brightness that radiated in waves from the pristine interior. And don't even get her started on the so-called "art" that hung on the walls . . .

"Hey," Sophie whispered excitedly in her ear, pointing one French-manicured index finger toward the far corner of the dance floor. "Isn't that *Drew* over there?"

Madison's gaze followed the trajectory of Sophie's finger, her green eyes narrowing further now in anger, as she caught sight of a suited Drew wrapped in what looked like a very intense embrace with some girl she'd never laid eyes on before in her life. The girl's hair fell down her back in loose waves, and Madison watched, incredulous, as Drew lifted his lips from hers and reached up to smooth her dark locks back from her face. A wave of anger mixed with jealousy so intense that she almost moaned aloud rushed through Madison's body, gluing her sandals to the floor, her feet suddenly unable to carry her forward.

"No. He. DIDN'T!" Sophie exclaimed, her cotton candy–colored mouth falling open in a wide O. "Who the hell is he *with*, anyway?" Sophie hissed hotly in her ear, the clean, citrusy scent of her Missoni perfume suddenly bringing on an enormous headache that felt like a pile driver slamming into Madison's skull, her stomach tumbling and turning beneath her Gucci dress.

Whatever, she told herself, willing her feet to move forward as she tossed her hair back from her shoulders. *Drew can date whoever he wants—and obviously that's exactly what he's doing.*

And two can definitely play that game, Mad told herself in a voice that was slightly more confident than she really felt. God, why couldn't she just get the hell over him once and for all? And why did she suddenly have the sneaking suspicion that Drew was really losing it? This kind of totally random behavior wasn't like him at *all*. Well, at least not that she knew of . . . But in any case, it was obvious that the guy she *thought* she knew was long gone.

"I have no idea," she answered in her best I-could-give-a-flying-fuck tone of voice. "But I *definitely* need a drink."

"For realz," Sophie agreed with a roll of her bottle-green eyes. "Jesus," she said thoughtfully with a small giggle, "I thought I was *hallucinating* there for a minute!"

As they made their way through the crowded room, Madison caught sight of Casey standing over by the edge of the dance floor with Darin. Casey was wearing Phoebe's cobalt blue Marni dress that was so totally two years ago, and laughing with the eternally irritating Emo boy, Mr. Hollingsworth, whose poster-child, relief-fund physique was tucked into the skinniest Gucci suit Mad had ever seen, a white Sex Pistols T-shirt peeking out from beneath the tight black blazer, black Converse high-tops on his feet.

"Shouldn't you be home putting coal in everyone's stocking?" Madison asked sarcastically as they approached. "Or writing Conor Oberst your millionth fan e-mail?"

"Oh, I'm *sorry*," Darin answered with an amused grin, feigning surprise. "I didn't recognize you without the *latte* in your hand." Sophie burst out laughing, bringing one hand up to her mouth in order to hide her grin. Madison glared at Darin, shooting him a tight smile that said "that's about as much of your shit as I'm prepared to take" written all over it. Darin looked over at Sophie and tilted his head upward in greeting. "What's up, Sophs?"

"Not much," Sophie answered after she'd gotten a hold of herself, craning her neck up as far as it could go so she could scan the crowd, the square-cut diamond studs in her ears sparkling in the light like melted ice cubes. "Have you guys seen Pheebs?"

"I think she's with Jared over there," Darin said, pointing in the general direction of the ice sculpture that was, despite the relentless blasts of air-conditioning chilling the room, rapidly beginning to melt. "I'm surprised you guys are all here. Isn't the big premiere tonight?"

"Don't remind me," Madison snapped. "I'm TiVoing it, of course, but it won't be the same as watching it *live*."

"Oh, of course not," Darin said sarcastically, rolling his eyes at the ceiling, his disdain clearly palpable.

"Glad we're all getting along so well." Casey laughed uncomfortably, putting one hand on Darin's arm as if to say "chill out." "C'mon," she said, tugging on Darin's sleeve as the string quartet finally stopped playing, and the DJ who'd been setting up at the front of the room for the better part of the last hour began to spin a hypnotic house track. "Let's all go dance."

"No thanks," Mad snapped, crossing her arms over her chest. "I think I'd rather drink battery acid."

"That can be arranged," Darin answered back. "The bar's over there—I'm sure if you snap your fingers, the bartender will run out and get you some."

Madison's eyes glowed a violent green as she took in Darin's smug expression. Did he really think he could compete with her? Didn't he know that when it came to any kind of verbal battle, she *always* won? Clearly, he had no idea who he was dealing with, but he was absolutely, unequivocally about to find out.

But before she could effectively tell Mr. Hollingsworth where exactly he could shove it, Madison glanced over at Casey, noticing that she had rapidly turned white, her face draining of color, her freckles standing out in high relief against her newly pale skin. Her gray eyes were focused on the dance floor, and Mad followed her gaze right to the flushed, happy face of Drew Van Allen, who was headed their way, his date trailing behind him, her white dress flowing at her feet like a puddle of softly whipped cream.

"What's up, Drew," Darin asked, holding out one hand so that Drew could slap his palm against it.

"Just hanging," Drew said, the smile sliding from his face as he surveyed the crowd, his eyes resting on Madison's face, then flitting away. The dark-haired girl sidled up beside him, reaching down and taking one of his hands in her own, squeezing tightly. Casey, Sophie, and Madison all followed Olivia's movements with their eyes as Drew began to squirm uncomfortably, shifting his weight from one foot to the other, his face betraying his obvious discomfort.

"Isn't he even going to *introduce* her?" Sophie leaned over and whispered in Mad's ear. Madison shrugged her bare shoulders, her gaze icy. Casey simply looked at the floor, her face deathly pale.

"So, how'd you do on that last calc test?" Darin asked, nonchalantly placing one arm around Casey's shoulders—an action that immediately caused Casey's pale visage to turn bright, strawberry red as she looked up, a vaguely panicked expression in her eyes.

"It kind of kicked my ass," Drew answered, looking uncomfortably from Darin's face to Mad's, then over to Casey's, his darkening gaze lingering on the arm that was now so casually draped across her shoulders.

"Do you go to Princeton, too?" Olivia asked brightly, her face open and eager to connect with the group. Mad looked at her smooth, creamy skin, her wavy dark hair, the Oscar de la Renta dress that floated around her slim figure, and hated her on sight. *Princeton?* Mad mused, narrowing her eyes at Drew and raising one darkened brow questioningly. *So, that's how you roll?*

Darin frowned, a look of confusion passing over his face as he turned wordlessly to Casey, who shrugged uncomprehendingly. "I go to Meadowlark Academy," Darin said slowly as a look of horror broke over Drew's face, the words spilling out before Darin completely understood his faux pas. "With Drew and these guys," Darin finished pointing at Casey, Mad, and then Sophie.

"Meadowlark?" Olivia said slowly, her eyes moving from

Drew back to Darin. "But isn't that . . . a *high school?*" Olivia wondered aloud as Madison watched with no small degree of satisfaction as a flush of heat rose up Drew's throat and settled in his cheeks. Olivia took a step back from Drew, looking at him questioningly, her expression one of confusion and disbelief.

"Olivia," Drew said, his voice rapidly bordering on frantic, "just let me explain." Drew ran a hand through his dark hair, which immediately made it stand on end as if he'd been electrocuted. "I wanted to—"

But before Drew could finish, Mad watched as Olivia's weirdly colored eyes turned stony and hard as she dropped Drew's hand from her own, staring at the appendage as if it were diseased, then turned her back on the group without another word. Mad watched with barely contained happiness as Olivia began to push through the crowded room toward the exit without stopping, or looking back. *Good*, Mad thought as she smoothed her hair back from her face with one practiced hand, watching as Drew's eyes followed Olivia's exit, his face collapsing like a fallen chocolate soufflé at Le Bernadin. *He's finally getting just what he deserves.*

Madison Macallister thought religion was basically for wimps who didn't have the dual gods of bitterness and sarcasm to pray to nightly, and she certainly didn't go in for any kind of crunchy New Age bullshit that required lighting candles and babbling to statues that looked more like garden gnomes than actual religious deities, but, nonetheless, she *was* a big believer in karma. And one thing Madison knew without a doubt was that whatever you put out there, you usually got back—tenfold. Unless, of course, you just happened to be Madison Macallister, who was usually exempt from such cosmic clusterfucks. And, as she stood there taking in the sudden derailment of Drew's very existence, she was more than just a little certain that at that very moment, Drew Van Allen was most *definitely* riding a massive wave of intense karmic payback. And payback, as everyone who paid even the lightest attention to the daily workings of the universe knew, was *always* a total bitch.

But then again, so am I, Madison thought triumphantly, as Drew walked quickly away from the group without speaking another word, his face a mask of anguish and disappointment.

crushed

Phoebe popped a miniature crab cake into her mouth and chewed rapidly, reaching for a toast point spread with goat cheese and sprinkled with balsamic vinegar, totally disgusted with herself for breaking her rule of never eating at parties, especially when there were cute guys around. And adding insult to injury was the fact that now her fingers were *totally* going to smell like fish all night . . . But she couldn't help it—she always got insanely hungry whenever she was nervous or confused, and right now she was definitely both. And if she wasn't careful, she was seriously going to pop right out of the Zac Posen white sheath dress she'd swiped from her mother's overstuffed closet . . .

"Do you want to dance?" Jared asked with a smile, leaning

closer and wrapping his arm tightly around her waist. Phoebe looked up into her boyfriend's gorgeous face, at his dark hair that was combed neatly back for a change instead of always flopping adorably in his eyes, at his glowing olive skin that made him appear as if he was perpetually on vacation, at the sleek gray Paul Sebastian suit that hugged his body like it had been designed especially for him, and waited to feel the usual jolt of lust begin in her stomach and spread through her limbs like warm, sticky taffy. But the only thing Phoebe felt was an ominous rumbling in her stomach that most likely meant that the crab cakes were *far* from fresh.

Ever since her coffee date with Drew the other night, Phoebe couldn't seem to stop thinking about him—the adorable dimple in his left cheek, his blue eyes that were full of so much uncertainty and pain, his muscular forearms that protruded from his hoodie when he absentmindedly pushed up the sleeves in the middle of their convo . . . Why had she never noticed how totally hot he was before? *Ummm, maybe because he was your best friend's boyfriend*, she told herself, reaching for another crab cake to drown out the crush-butterflies that stubbornly began to swoop around her stomach and flap their way up her chest at the very thought of Drew Van Allen, *and contraband*. It was like Jared—all over again. Was she only destined to crush on guys who were totally off limits, not to mention unavailable?

"Not yet," Phoebe answered, covering her mouth with one hand as she chewed, rolling her eyes in irritation. He was just being Jared, her boyfriend, doing boyfriend stuff like putting an arm around her and asking her to dance. So why did she feel like starting a huge, wicked fight for no reason and stomping off?

"Whatever," Jared said sulkily, removing his arm from around her waist, picking up his glass of champagne from the buffet table, and draining it in one swallow, clearly annoyed.

"Darling!" a high-pitched voice called out. Phoebe turned around just in time to see her mother striding toward them, her twiglike body swathed in the new silver Chanel couture gown she'd seen hanging on the back of Madeline's door earlier that evening. The silver fabric clung like droplets of water to her mother's body, accentuating her minuscule waist, and highlighting her creamy skin and dark hair. A diamond choker by Chopard sparkled around her neck, and a matching bracelet gleamed on one wrist. Phoebe's expression darkened as she took in the pair, remembering the party last year for her mother's thirty-eighth birthday when her father had presented her with the jewels in front of the whole crowd, the way Madeline had drawn him tenderly to her and kissed him as the crowd applauded.

"I've been looking for you simply everywhere!" Madeline said excitedly, resting one perfectly crimson manicured hand on Phoebe's arm, squeezing gently. Since Madeline usually wanted as little to do with her daughter as possible, Madeline's behavior began to worry Phoebe almost immediately.

"Why?" Phoebe said suspiciously, picking up another toast

point and crunching down on it voraciously, relishing the loud, inappropriate sound the dry toast made breaking between her teeth.

"Hey, Mrs. Reynaud," Jared interrupted, leaning in and kissing Madeline quickly on both cheeks.

"Jared," Madeline purred with obvious pleasure, pursing her lips flirtatiously. "Are you back from school already?"

"I'm just taking a bit of a break," Jared answered, his cheeks flushing as the words left his lips.

Phoebe rolled her eyes and snorted aloud before she could put herself in check. Jared had been tossed out of Exeter at the beginning of the year, for reasons that no one could seem to figure out. And no matter how many times she asked outright, or loosened *this* strap, or *that* button, Jared had kept his silence about the whole affair.

"Phoebe," Madeline went on excitedly, "I just spoke to Andrea, and she informed me that if you really start taking your extracurricular activities seriously, that you have a solid shot at Harvard's International Business program! Isn't that exciting?" Madeline's blue eyes sparkled, and Phoebe couldn't help but wonder what it would be like growing up with a mother who was physically demonstrative *all* the time—not just as a reward whenever her daughter acted like the perfect little designer-clad android who said and did all the right things without question.

"Yeah, I guess," Phoebe answered slowly. "But what about fashion? You know that I want to be a *designer*—not some international banker!"

"We've already had this conversation, Phoebe," Madeline said flatly, her eyes hardening as she spoke.

"I'm *aware* of that," Phoebe blurted out, feeling her pulse begin to race the way it always did when she was feeling out of control, the vein in her forehead that always stuck out pounding away. "That's the problem. You're not *listening* to me!"

"Hey, Pheebs," Jared said softly, touching her arm, "it's not like Harvard is exactly punishment, right? And I'll come visit you every weekend." Jared smiled, ready, as always, to make light of the whole situation. But Phoebe had had enough of sweeping everything messy under the carpet, enough of doing what she was told, just because it might make a scene to simply refuse. She was so tired of *not* making a scene that she felt like her head was going to explode. Phoebe stared at Jared incredulously. How dare he take Madeline's side and not her own? Especially after everything he knew about the Reynauds' recent family drama? How *could* he?

"Exactly," Madeline said smugly, reaching up and patting her hair, which was arranged in a complicated French roll at the back of her head, completely ignoring Phoebe's outburst. "Now, I'll leave you two lovebirds alone," she trilled with a wave of her hand. "So *good* to see you, Jared." Madeline shot Jared a conspiratorial smile, reaching over to kiss him on the cheek before sailing off in a cloud of Serge Lutens perfume. Phoebe whirled around to face Jared, unable to keep her anger in check a second longer.

"How *could* you?" she hissed, her hands balled into fists at her side, her nails digging into her palms with such force that she almost cried out. "How could you take her *side*?"

"I wasn't taking her side," Jared said calmly, reaching over to the table, grabbing a crab cake and popping it thoughtfully into his mouth. "It's just less of a hassle if you just learn to agree, you know? I mean," he went on, chewing and swallowing, "the best way to deal with the shit our parents throw at us is just to nod and smile—and *then* go do exactly what you want anyway."

"That's the stupidest thing I've ever heard!" Phoebe snapped, pushing her hair, which she had worn loose that night, from her face where it was currently sticking to her bronze Hard Candy lip gloss.

"If you say so," Jared said mildly, refusing to engage in the argument, which made Phoebe madder than ever. "C'mon," he said, pulling Phoebe closer and wrapping an arm around her waist once again—an arm she promptly shook off. "Are you going to be in a bad mood all *night* now?"

"Count on it," Phoebe snapped, glaring at Jared like she was trying to burn holes in his perfect, tawny skin, and walked off toward the bathroom, afraid if she stood there for one more minute that she'd say something she might regret later. As she made her way through the crowd, Phoebe caught sight of Drew standing at the bar alone, downing one glass of champagne after another, his face set with concentration. Phoebe's heart leapt in her chest, a smile breaking the frown that had spread across her face ever since Madeline had made her appearance. All at once she felt almost . . . happy. But as her feet moved toward him on autopilot, she was stopped suddenly in her tracks by the reality of the situation. Drew wasn't her boyfriend—Jared was. Drew was, well, *Drew*, who had belonged to Madison, then Casey, and now, who knew? And that simple equation meant he was utterly off limits. Sophie may have finally forgiven her for getting involved with Jared, her own brother, but Phoebe knew that over the years Madison Macallister had broken the world's record for holding a grudge—more than once.

Forget about him, she told herself, redirecting her path and walking again toward the bathroom. *And concentrate on the boyfriend you do have. Until the other night you were madly in lust with him, right?*

"Right," Phoebe answered aloud with a sigh as she pushed through the swinging door of the ladies' room, and stood in front of the heavily lighted mirror, gazing intently at her own reflection. If Madeline had her way, Phoebe knew that she might never find out who she was, or what she could become. And as she stared at her reflection in the silver glass, Phoebe Reynaud knew that despite whatever she felt or didn't feel about Drew and Jared, she was never, ever going to willfully pack away her own dreams for anyone else's benefit.

revelations

"I'll be right back, " Casey said, squirming out from under Darin's arm, which was draped over her shoulders, and walked toward the bar, where Drew was currently auditioning for the next season of *Intervention*, as he methodically slammed back one glass of champagne after another. Everyone in the group seemed content to let him walk away after his date had run off. Sophie and Mad had immediately started giggling and whispering, and Darin had just stood there with his arm around Casey's shoulders, not saying much of anything at all. But once Casey had taken in the look on Drew's face, the disappointment and heartache that had dulled his blue eyes, there was no way she could stand there and watch him attempt to drink all the champagne on the Upper East Side without at least going over to see if he was okay.

"Where are *you* going?" Madison asked coolly, imperiously raising an eyebrow, her expression and tone both implying that Casey was a fool for even considering such a thing. "You should just let him suffer."

Casey hesitated for a minute, realizing that by going over there and talking to Drew, she was putting her newfound friendship with Madison—if she could really call it that—in total jeopardy. But was that really the kind of person she wanted to be? Someone who turned their back on a friend just to fit in? And Casey knew, just from looking at the way no one seemed in any hurry to rush to Drew's aid, that the answer was a clear and resounding no.

"That's not really my style," Casey answered, looking meaningfully at Madison, and walking away before the green-eyed icon could end the conversation with one of her highly effective sarcastic retorts.

As she approached, Drew looked up, placing his empty champagne flute back on the bar and grabbing a refill. Casey walked over to the bar with the pretext of getting some champagne for herself, her heart fluttering erratically beneath Phoebe's blue dress, which scratched against her skin like sheets of gorgeously blue sandpaper.

"Hey," she said quietly, wrapping her fingers around the stem of the glass in her hand for reassurance. "Are you okay?"

Drew looked up, his eyes, so blue and usually full of life,

now flat and lifeless. "Not really," he answered in a voice that sounded more mechanical than human. "Not at all, actually."

"You told her you go to Princeton?" Casey asked tentatively, not sure if asking was the right thing to do, but too curious to stop herself.

"Yeah," Drew said disgustedly, draining his glass and placing it down on the bar, shoving his hands in his pockets. "Smart, huh?"

"Why?" Casey asked, her gray eyes filled with confusion. She didn't want to believe that the first guy she'd seriously fallen for was just a liar, an opportunist.

"I don't know," Drew said with a sigh, his eyes sweeping the room. Watching him, Casey got the feeling that it really bothered him to have to talk about this while simultaneously looking at her face. "I wanted things to be different. I thought that if I gave myself some other life, that somehow things would be easier. I'm an idiot." Drew's voice broke slightly on the last word, and Casey felt her own heart begin to break along with it.

"No," Casey said urgently, unable to stop herself from reaching out and touching his arm gently, the feel of his warm body beneath his jacket practically sending her into a swoon, despite what she'd just witnessed, despite Darin, despite the exceedingly sticky situation that had gone down between Drew and Madison only a week ago. In spite of everything she knew and everything she *didn't*, all Casey was sure of was the fact that she couldn't deny the complicated, rhythmic music her own heart made whenever Drew was in the immediate vicinity. "You're *not*."

"Right," Drew said sarcastically, moving away from her touch and running a hand through his hair distractedly. "It's just, all this stuff has been going on with my parents—and I guess I'm pretty screwed up about it." Drew swallowed hard and looked out at the happy couples crowding the dance floor.

"What *happened*?" Casey asked tentatively, fighting her impulse to wrap her arms around him and tell him that everything would be okay, no matter what it was that had happened. But despite her urge to try to fix the situation with physical contact, Casey knew that it wasn't what Drew needed right then. And besides, Drew wasn't hers anymore—if he had ever been in the first place—and that being said, all she could really do for him was to listen to whatever he had to say.

"My dad's having an affair with Phoebe's mom—I caught them practically making out at Sophie's party." Drew practically spit out the words, wiping his mouth with the back of his hand immediately afterward, as if they disgusted him completely.

"*That's* why you ran out?" Casey said incredulously, the realization that Drew's behavior had nothing to do with her rushing through her brain, confusing everything she thought she'd understood about the two of them.

"Yeah," Drew said, looking over, a sheepish expression on his face. "I didn't know how to deal with it. I just had to get out of there."

"But why didn't you call me *after*?" Casey wondered aloud, her eyes full of confusion.

"I didn't know what to say," Drew answered, his eyes full of regret. "I mean, you're from *Normal*, for God's sake." Drew looked out over the dance floor again as the music shifted to a dreamy, lush track that made Casey think of romance, roses, and kisses—all the things that she shouldn't have been thinking of at that very moment. "How could you possibly understand my joke of a family when yours is so perfect?"

"Perfect?" Casey repeated, completely stunned by Drew's admission. "Where the hell did you get *that* idea?" Drew opened his mouth to speak, gesturing with one hand in the air, but before he could find the words, Casey rushed on, cutting off the possibility. "My parents divorced when I was thirteen," she said angrily, "and my mom basically dumped me here so that she could spend the year in London without any distractions. Does that sound *perfect* to you?"

"I guess not," Drew said with a small smile, turning to face her. "So, are you trying to tell me that *you're* not perfect then either?"

"Far from it," Casey retorted with a snort. "But, if you'll remember, I've already *told* you that before—and even if I hadn't, it should be pretty obvious by now."

Drew exhaled heavily, his blue eyes meeting hers. "Not to me," he said quietly, deliberately.

Casey felt her pulse quicken again, adrenaline rushing through her body like a derailed freight train lumbering across the tracks. Suddenly she felt shaky, like she'd been mainlining

Diet Cokes all night long instead of Veuve Clicquot. Drew reached out, his eyes glassy with feeling, and placed her hand in his own. Casey turned around briefly to look at the group she'd left behind, standing right where she'd left them and staring unabashedly. A look of disgust broke over Darin's face as he took in the sight of Casey's hand entwined in Drew's. At the exact same moment, Madison leaned over to Sophie, cupping her hand around her ear and whispering furiously, her green eyes never straying from Casey's, her feline face blank and impassive.

"I should get back," Casey said unsteadily, turning to look back at Drew, who was looking at her intently now, seemingly unwilling to relinquish her hand.

"Can I call you?" Drew asked quietly, squeezing her fingers tightly in his own before releasing her hand.

Casey looked down at her still-tingling fingers, her mind flooded with unanswered questions that danced through her brain in a demented conga line, confusing her endlessly. Why couldn't she be more like Madison and make Drew grovel, the way he probably deserved to? Why did she want to scream YES at the top of her lungs the minute the question fell from his lips? *Maybe because you have no self-respect,* her inner dating Nazi said smugly, crossing its arms over its chest.

Or maybe, Casey answered back defiantly, *I just really, really like him. And, besides—everyone deserves a second chance, even Drew Van Allen.*

"Yeah," she answered finally, unable to stop herself from smiling happily as she spoke, her face beginning to glow as brightly as the circular white walls that surrounded them. "I think I'd really like that." And when Drew smiled back, something in Casey's torn heart began suddenly to mend, the disappointment and regret she'd carried with her for the last six weeks disappearing in the electricity that rose up into the air, closing the space in between their two lone bodies.

de-luxe

Madison watched as Drew took Casey's hand in his own, an intense, pleading expression contorting his handsome face, and indignation begin to rise like an electric swarm of fireflies lighting up the hollow cavity of her chest. If anyone deserved to be on the receiving end of both apologies *and* hand-holding, Madison knew without a doubt that it was her—not some total sap who would probably forgive Drew for all of his endlessly rude, irritating bullshit in less than ten seconds flat. Madison stared at the way Casey's silky hair now fell well past her shoulders, at the blue dress that hugged her slim frame like a roll of wrapping paper, and as she took it all in, Madison knew that when it came to looks, there was really no contest—she was prettier. By *far.* So, if it wasn't looks, then what *was* it that kept Drew going back to Casey time and time again? The more Mad stood there, trying to figure it out, the more confused she became, a sudden, blinding pain cutting through her skull like a sliver of light slicing through a dark room.

"Well, *that's* an interesting development," Sophie said aloud, crossing her arms over her chest as Casey began to walk across the room toward them, a dreamy expression plastered over her lightly freckled face. "I mean, what was that all *about*, anyway?" Sophie added questioningly.

"What was all that bullshit Drew was spewing about Princeton?" Darin wondered aloud, shaking his head from side to side in disbelief. "And who *was* that girl, anyway?"

"Who knows," Mad said, her voice shaking with anger despite her best efforts to seem cool and collected, as if she couldn't care less. "And who cares." Sophie just shrugged, knowing better than to press the subject when Madison was this pissed off. Madison focused in on Casey as she approached, her gaze as determined as a laser beam, her irritation clearly visible. As Casey walked up, shooting all three of them an apologetic smile, Mad tossed her hair back from her shoulders and lifted her head high. Just because Drew was acting like a moron once again didn't mean she had to stand there and take it. Besides, once the show began to air regularly, Mad knew that it would only be a matter of time before Casey was privy to the glorious footage of her and Drew's frantic make-out session at Space. And once Casey saw Drew's lips locked to her own in living color, Madison knew that it wouldn't be long before Ms. Normal's rampant insecurity would soon be making a guest appearance. But, until then, Madison definitely wasn't going to stand there and act like everything was sunshine and flowers when it was decidedly *not*.

"I'm leaving," Mad said forcefully, her lips drawn into an icy smile, her fingers wrapped so tightly around her black patent leather Dior clutch that she was afraid they were about to snap off from the pressure.

"I'll go with you," Sophie said with a sigh as she turned toward Casey. "This party's even more boring than last year."

"I'll go with you guys," Casey said brightly, looking over at Darin and smiling, obviously looking for the green light from her "date."

Some date, Madison thought darkly, narrowing her eyes at Darin, who seemed irritatingly oblivious to the fact that Drew Van Allen had just basically fallen all over himself for the opportunity to hold Casey's hand. A wave of pain rushed through Madison's body, sweeping through her torso with such force that she almost bent over from the intensity of it. If she didn't really care about Drew the way she'd been telling herself for the past two years, then why did it feel like her heart was being ripped from her chest with a pair of barbecue tongs? Why did she want to go home and spoon ice cream into her mouth until she could feel nothing but icy numbness, until her extremities were deadened by first the cold, then the subsequent sugar rush, which would lead her, she knew, into dead, dreamless sleep?

"That's really not necessary," Madison snapped, turning her back on Casey and stepping determinedly through the crowd. Mad knew that if she didn't get out of that room, if she didn't keep moving one stiletto in front of the other, she was going to go back there and say something to Drew that she'd undoubtedly be very sorry for later, when she got control of her emotions. *It's just Drew Van Allen,* she told herself as she pushed through the crowd. *Why do you even care?*

But no matter how many times she repeated the words in her spinning brain, the answer that rose to the surface was always the same—six words that stopped her heart dead in its tracks as they made their way from the confines of her throat, and up to her lips, where they spilled into the air.

"Because I'm in love with him," Mad murmured in disbelief, coming to a dead stop in the middle of the dance floor, and clapping her hand over her mouth to stifle the words, the bass pumping up from the floor and through her body, her limbs buzzing with the potent combination of music and truth. *Oh my God.* Madison raised a hand to her forehead and rested one palm lightly against her skin, as if checking for fever. *Am I sick,* she wondered wordlessly. *Maybe someone spiked my champagne . . .* Against her better judgment, Madison couldn't help but question the feelings coursing through her heart with the intensity of a just-released bottle rocket into the night sky. Could it really be true? *Was* she in love with Drew Van Allen? When exactly had things shifted from just a game to *anything* even remotely approaching realness? Madison didn't know the answer, or what, if anything, she was going to do about this revelation. All she *did* know was that for the first time in her life, she was absolutely, positively head over heels in love, and that the feeling hurt more than anything she'd ever experienced—worse than a bikini wax at J. Sisters, worse than micro-dermabrasion, worse than watching Edie and Antonio make out like a pair of nauseating, lovesick morons. Because despite sleeping with her, despite chasing her around the entire Upper East Side for the last two years, Madison knew with a finality that tore her chest in two that Drew didn't love her back—that he loved *Casey*. Casey, with all of her glaring imperfections, was the one Drew had chosen. Not her.

And it was fucking killing her.

"Mad! Wait!" Madison felt a rush of air at her back as Sophie hurled herself at Madison's body like a human projectile, her hands resting lightly on Madison's semi-bare back. "I'm totally going with you."

"Me, too," a small voice piped up.

Mad turned around and was greeted by the face of the one person she wished would simply evaporate from the planet without explanation. Casey McCloy stood behind Sophie, offering up a tentative smile while worriedly gnawing at her bottom lip. *She should be worried*, Madison mused, wishing they both would just leave her alone for a change. *Because when I get through with her, she's going to wish she were dead—or at least comatose.*

"Oh my God," Sophie exclaimed, linking her arm through Madison's and moving toward the front door of the museum, "let's go to my house and watch the premiere on TiVo!"

"Whatever," Madison snapped. "I just want to get out of here. I have a headache so bad it feels like a fucking aneurysm."

"Maybe you have Alzheimer's." Casey giggled as they reached the exit.

Madison snorted, pushing her way out the revolving glass door, turning around slightly to shoot Casey a look that would freeze water in the Sahara. "Maybe you should shut up," Madison said sweetly, her voice as frigid as the icicles hanging from the tops of the buildings on Fifth Avenue.

As Madison pushed her way out the door, pulling her coat around her body and relishing the cold air that slapped her in the face like a frozen cashmere scarf, her vision was clouded by a barrage of white lights, camera flashes going off in front of her with a sudden violence that approximated a physical assault. Madison put a hand up in front of her face as she squinted her green eyes, trying to focus on the scene, which was suddenly splotched with pink-and-white dots that swam across the surface of her vision, making it impossible to focus her gaze.

"There they are!" one reporter yelled out, and, with that, the crowd surged forward and enveloped Mad, Sophie, and Casey, who hid behind Sophie's tiny body, peeking out like a little kid on Christmas morning.

This is it, Madison told herself, rolling the words around in her mind triumphantly. She squared her shoulders, tilting her chin imperiously, bathing in the flashes of white light, and with one fluid motion, Madison dropped her coat to the floor, exposing her barely-there Gucci dress, and posed, one hand on her cocked hip. *I may have struck out with Drew*, Mad thought, smiling widely and exposing rows of teeth equal in intensity to the brilliant white lights that surrounded them. *But nothing is going to get in the way of this moment . . .*

"Casey!" one reporter yelled out. "Where's Casey Mc-Cloy?"

Madison felt her blood run as cold as an anaconda's, her gaze hardening as Casey's name rang out into the brisk winter air, her frozen hands dropping from her hips and curling tightly into fists.

"Here she is!" Sophie said brightly, pushing Casey in front of Madison and into the spotlight. Casey squinted, holding up one hand before her gray eyes to try to shield her face from the barrage of lights.

Madison glared incredulously at Sophie, who seemed oblivious as she stood there positively beaming like Casey was her own *child. No she DIDN'T!* Madison fumed silently as she tried to twist her sour face into anything that even remotely resembled a smile.

"Casey!" a female reporter from the E! channel shouted out, pushing through the crowd and shoving a microphone into Casey's stunned face, her bright red lipstick shining glossily, the light glinting off her Armani frames. "How does it feel to be the new It Girl of the Upper East Side?"

Madison froze, her mouth falling open as the first snowfall of the winter began to drift lazily down from the sky, the flakes sticking in her lashes and coating the top of her head. Casey? An It Girl? Had the reporters lost what was left of their freakin' minds? Couldn't they see that Casey was just some annoying dork from the Midwest? That she was as much of an It Girl as Paris Hilton was a member of Mensa? *This isn't happening*, Madison told herself, as the reporters swarmed around Casey like hundreds of busily buzzing bees, the questions shouted out into the night air fading into nothing more than an insistent drone that filled Madison's ears and made her suddenly light-headed. *I must be dreaming.*

Madison reached down and pinched her bare arm hard, closing her eyes as her nails dug into her flesh. But when she opened them again, the lights and reporters were still there. And, worse yet, it was Casey McCloy who was basking in the halogen glare like it was a tanning bed, tilting her lightly freckled face up to the light and smiling brilliantly, her wide grin reflected endlessly in the transparent surface of the lens, and the crowd surged forward once again, swallowing her up completely.

Printed in the United States
by Baker & Taylor Publisher Services